Norse Star

By Jeff Mildon

Printed in the United States of America
ISBN: 978-1-968360-00-9
Imprint: MiltyMedia

First Printing, 202

Contents

Chapter 1: The Encounter

The fjords of Norway unfurled in every direction, jagged cliffs rising from dark waters like the teeth of slumbering giants. Overhead, the moon hung low, a pale silver disc casting ghostly reflections that shimmered across the sea. The dark waters reflected the heavens, a mirror to the world above, broken only by the slow ripple of the longships cutting through the sea's surface.

The moon hung low, a pale silver disc suspended over the black abyss, its dim glow stretching long, ghostly fingers across the water. The aurora borealis twisted above, writhing like a celestial serpent, shifting in unnatural hues of green, blue, and violet. The colors burned, vibrant yet eerie, illuminating the sea and casting an otherworldly glow upon the men who sailed beneath it.

The longships of Erik Bloodaxe's fleet glided silently, their dragon-headed prows gleaming under the flickering light.

And yet, Something was wrong.

The usual symphony of the ocean was absent—no rhythmic slapping of waves against the hull, no creak of the wooden planks as they flexed under the wind. Even the gulls that followed them from distant shores had disappeared, their cries swallowed by the stillness.

No wind carried between the cliffs. No distant howl of wolves from the forests beyond. Even the shadows felt heavier, like unseen eyes pressed against the edges of reality, watching, waiting. It was as if the world itself had paused, holding its breath for something unseen.

At the prow of Stormfang, Erik Bloodaxe stood like a statue of war, his silhouette framed by the unnatural light dancing across the heavens. His thick auburn beard, streaked with frost, moved only slightly with the motion of the ship. His grip tightened on the haft of his great axe, his knuckles whitening beneath the wolf-fur bracers that lined his wrists.

He was no stranger to war, to death, to the unknown. He had raided the halls of kings, fought battles beneath the banners of Saxons and Franks, and spilled blood on every land his longships had touched. Yet this night unnerved him in a way no battlefield ever had.

The cold was unnatural, biting deeper than any winter's wind. It gnawed at the edges of his furs, seeped into his very bones, as though something unseen reached for him, clawing through the darkness.

Behind him, his warriors stirred, their unease as tangible as the frost in the air. These were not men easily shaken.

They had braved oceans so fierce that even the gods might tremble. They had stood atop the burning remains of monasteries; blades soaked in the blood of those who called upon Christ instead of Odin. They had torn riches from the hands of cowards and forged their fates with steel and fire. And yet, they clutched their weapons tightly tonight.

Torvald the Elder, a man with more scars than unbroken skin, gritted his teeth and spat into the sea. The black water swallowed his offering without a ripple, as if the ocean itself refused to acknowledge them.

His weathered face twisted with suspicion as he wrapped his thick fingers around the hilt of his sword.

"This silence is an ill omen, Erik."

His voice was a low growl, a whisper that barely dared to break the unnatural quiet.

"The gods whisper through the winds, but tonight, they have fallen silent."

Bjorn Stonehand, a mountain of a man, ran his fingers along the edge of his axe.

"Then let them watch." His voice was gruff, yet there was an edge to it that betrayed his unease. "If battle comes, we will carve our names into the bones of the world."

Gunnar the Red, younger than most, barely past his twentieth winter, rubbed his thumb against the iron amulet of Thor that hung around his neck.

"This night is cursed."

He clenched his fists as though he could squeeze the fear from his blood. He had heard the stories all his life, of his father, a shield-brother of Erik Bloodaxe, who had fallen on a foreign shore. Gunnar had trained to live up to that name, to earn the respect it carried. But now, facing something no saga had ever described, he felt that legacy wrap around his throat like a noose.

The warriors exchanged uneasy glances, but none dared speak louder than a whisper. The quiet was too thick, pressing against their senses like a storm yet to break.

Erik turned his gaze toward the distant ice-capped mountains, their white peaks reflecting the shimmering auroras. The sky above had always been alive—the lights shifting in slow, dreamlike patterns, a dance of the gods above.

But tonight, the lights twisted differently. They spun like a great spiral, bending and stretching as though being pulled toward something unseen. The colors bled together unnaturally, churning like a storm trapped between the heavens and the earth.

It was a movement he had never seen before. A movement that did not belong. Then, it happened.

At first, it was just a glimmer, a subtle flicker amidst the celestial flames overhead. But then, without warning, a searing column of light erupted from the sky, a lance of emerald fire piercing the heavens.

It swelled, pulsing, like the heartbeat of the gods, before exploding outward in a burst of pure radiance. The auroras convulsed. The sky twisted. The sea itself trembled beneath the weight of something immense.

The warriors shouted, staggering as the longships lurched. The unnatural force pushed against the water, bending reality itself as the sound of a great hum filled the air. Not the voice of thunder. Not the song of the winds. Something older. Something deeper.

Erik gritted his teeth, forcing himself to remain steady as the vibrations rattled his bones. And then, from the heart of the light, something descended.

A shape, vast and unholy, emerging from the void. It moved with a grace that defied the laws of the world, gliding without sails, without oars, without wind. It was unlike any ship ever crafted by mortal hands. The air crackled. The sea hissed. The silence that had gripped the world shattered, replaced by a presence too great to comprehend.

Torvald's breath hitched. His grip tightened on his sword.

"By the gods," he whispered.

Bjorn, for the first time in his life, made the sign of Thor's hammer across his chest. Gunnar stumbled backward, his eyes wide with terror.

"It is Jörmungandr," he choked out. "The end times are upon us."

Erik did not move. He simply watched, the light burning into his retinas as the impossible ship descended toward the sea.

Something older than the gods had come to Midgard. And there would be no turning back.

A sudden, blinding light exploded across the sky, turning the deep black of night into a blinding day. The heavens convulsed, a pulse of emerald and sapphire fire tearing through the sky like the blazing heart of a dying god.

The auroras writhed violently, their once gentle, ghostly dance transforming into a maelstrom of chaos, their colors bleeding together in a storm of shifting hues. They twisted into unnatural shapes, spiraling downward like a celestial vortex, its center pulling toward the waters below.

Then came the sound. A deafening hum, neither thunder nor wind, but something else entirely. It was deeper, older, vibrating with a force that shook the very bones of every man aboard the longships. It did not come from the earth, nor the heavens, but from somewhere beyond both.

The warriors cried out in shock, some throwing their hands over their eyes, others gripping their weapons with white-knuckled hands as if bracing for the wrath of the gods themselves.

Even the sea reacted, the once glassy black waters now trembling with unseen force, sending tiny waves rippling away from the center of the storm.

Then, from the heart of the twisting auroras, a shape emerged. It descended slowly, moving with unnatural grace, defying the very laws of the world itself.

The warriors watched in horrified awe as a massive vessel, gleaming like blackened steel, lowered from the heavens. It did not fall like a rock, nor drift like a feather, but instead moved with the measured intent of a living thing, its smooth surface gleaming beneath the swirling fires of the sky.

The air grew thick, the weight of something immense pressing down upon them, though not with the force of wind or wave. It was like the presence of a god, an unseen force that sent a thrumming pulse through the air and sea alike.

It touched the water. But no waves formed. No ripple disturbed the fjord's surface. The great vessel settled upon the sea as if the water itself bowed in reverence.

A hush fell over the fleet. The only sound was the thrumming hum, vibrating through wood, water, and bone, a song that did not belong to the earthly realm. The warriors stared in mute horror, their instincts screaming to run, to fight, to do anything but stand in the presence of this impossible thing.

Erik's hand tightened around his axe, his pulse pounding in his ears. His breath was slow and deliberate, but even he felt the ice of something far worse than fear creeping up his spine. Torvald was the first to speak, his voice barely a whisper over the hum.

"By the gods," he rasped, his breath visible in the cold night air.

The glow from the massive vessel illuminated the fjord, casting long shadows over the towering cliffs. The light was not like fire, nor the sun, but something colder, something not of this world.

Bjorn Stonehand's fingers twitched against the haft of his axe. He said nothing, at first. He rarely did, not until the blood had settled. But his eyes, cold as the fjord itself, scanned the beings before them. He was already calculating height, reach, and movement. They weren't berserkers. They were worse. Controlled.

"This is no ship," he muttered, his voice hoarse.

Erik narrowed his eyes, taking in the impossible smoothness of the vessel's surface. It had no seams, no planks, no sails. There were no oars, yet it glided effortlessly. No man had built this, nor had any god he had ever known.

Gunnar clutched his iron amulet.

"Jörmungandr," he whispered, his voice barely audible. "The great serpent has risen from the depths."

The name sent a ripple of dread through the warriors, as though the very mention of the World Serpent had given it power.

"Jörmungandr brings Ragnarok," another warrior muttered. His knuckles whitened as he clutched his spear, his lips moving in a hurried prayer to Odin.

But Erik wasn't so sure. Jörmungandr was the great beast, the bringer of chaos, the one who would rise from the depths at the end of all things.

But this...

This was not a beast. It was a ship. But not like any ship he had ever known. It did not creak under the weight of the sea. It did not rock with the waves. It floated like a shadow. A vessel carved from the void itself.

Erik gritted his teeth, the icy fingers of unease pressing against the back of his mind. He had fought kings, raided empires, and conquered lands across the sea—but this? This was beyond even the wildest battle songs of the skalds.

The hum deepened, vibrating through the very marrow of his bones. Then, the vessel moved. Not by oar. Not by sail. It glided forward smoothly, silently, and effortlessly. As though the fjord itself parted before it, bending to its presence.

The warriors staggered back, some gripping the sides of their longships as the great vessel drew closer. Its surface, dark and gleaming like polished obsidian, pulsed with lines of soft blue light, symbols flickering along its edges.

A low murmur spread through the warriors, some whispering prayers, others merely staring in paralyzed horror.

"It cannot be..." Torvald exhaled.

But it was. It was here. And the world would never be the same.

The world stood frozen, not just in silence, but in a moment of impossible reckoning.

Then, without warning, a portion of the ship's surface shifted, as though the metal itself were alive. A hatch opened silently, revealing a long, luminous ramp of pure light extending downward toward the water.

Then, they appeared. The warriors aboard Erik's ships staggered back as tall, slender figures emerged from the glowing ramp. They moved without sound, their steps too fluid, too precise to be natural.

The beings that descended the ramp moved with an effortless grace that defied human motion. They were humanoid, but… not human. Their forms were tall and slender. Their features were eerily perfect, their skin smooth and gleaming with a silver sheen. Their eyes glowed, reflecting the auroras above, as if they carried the stars within them. They wore robes of shifting material, fabric that flowed like water, changing color with every movement. The air around them shimmered, warping slightly, as though reality itself struggled to contain their presence. Their faces were neither grotesque nor entirely human, but strikingly symmetrical, their high cheekbones and elongated eyes exuding an unnatural presence. Their skin gleamed like polished metal, smooth and flawless, reflecting the faint glow of the auroras above.

Their leader, a figure standing at least a head taller than Erik, stepped forward. A soft glow emanated from beneath its robe, the source unclear. It stopped a few feet from the

Viking warband, studying them with those piercing, liquid-silver eyes.

Torvald's grip tightened on the hilt of his blade, callused fingers trembling, not from fear, but from memory. He had once watched a seer burn alive for speaking of fire from the stars. He had buried that vision in silence ever since. And now it walked toward him.

The warriors tensed. Hands clenched hilts, shields were adjusted, and breaths were held. The hum in Erik's bones grew stronger. Then, without moving their lips, a voice spoke inside his mind.

"Erik Bloodaxe, King of the North, you are known to us."

A collective gasp rippled through the warriors. Some clutched their weapons, others whispered prayers to Odin and Thor, their hands shaking. Erik did not move. His heart thundered, but he stood his ground.

"You speak my name as if we are old friends," Erik said, his voice steady despite the pounding of his heart. "Who are you?"

The tallest of the figures lifted a six-fingered hand and gestured toward Erik, palm upturned. A swirl of blue light coalesced in his palm, forming intricate symbols, like runes carved on Viking shields, that pulsed with an energy.

"We are the Zepharians," the figure said, his voice as deep as the void between stars. "And we bring you knowledge beyond the stars."

The fjord, the night, and the very air itself seemed to hold its breath. The Vikings stood at the precipice of a destiny they could not yet fathom. Torvald gripped his axe tightly, his knuckles turning white as he locked eyes with the glowing silver gaze of the Zepharian. Every fiber of his being told him to strike, to kill, to send this sorcerer from the sky back to whatever hell had birthed it.

The other warriors stood motionless, their breath visible in the cold air, hanging like mist between them and the impossible being that stood before them. The only sound was the distant lapping of water against the hulls of the longships, but even the sea itself seemed subdued, as if afraid to disturb the moment.

Torvald spoke. "Knowledge beyond the stars? Trickery." His voice was low, edged with suspicion. "No man speaks through the mind unless he deals in sorcery."

The Zepharian tilted its head, the motion smooth, effortless, almost too perfect. The glowing silver eyes flickered, like shifting pools of liquid light. The expression was not one of hostility or fear. It was curiosity.

"You see magic where there is only understanding."

The voice did not come from its lips, yet it rang clearly within Erik's mind. A shudder ran through the warriors. Some clutched their weapons, others took small, hesitant steps back. No one spoke, but their expressions screamed their thoughts.

Erik stepped forward, breaking the spell of fear that gripped his men. He had stood before kings and warlords, had watched the light fade from the eyes of enemies he had slain. He had faced death itself. But never had he faced something like this. This was not a man. Not a beast. Not a god. And yet, it stood before him, speaking his name, knowing his people.

His instincts screamed at him, telling him this was no enemy to be taken lightly. But neither was it something he could turn away from. If what they claimed was true... If they carried the wisdom of the heavens themselves...

Erik exhaled slowly, his grip relaxing slightly on his axe.

"What is it you seek?" he demanded. "No man gives knowledge without expecting something in return."

The Zepharian's glowing eyes did not waver.

"We seek nothing but to share."

The warriors shifted uneasily.

"Your kind is... unique among those we have encountered. Your ambition, your ferocity, your will to conquer against all odds. We have watched your people grow from the shadows of time."

A murmur ran through the warriors. Some of them looked to Erik, waiting for his response. Others did not hide their unease.

Gunnar, the youngest of them, his wild red hair tousled by the wind, spat onto the ice-slicked deck.

"This is folly!" he snarled. "We should not listen to whispers of ghosts!"

His voice was bold, but there was fear beneath it. To the Vikings, there were only two kinds of beings that could command such unnatural power, gods and monsters. And these beings were neither.

Torvald turned to Erik, his brow furrowed with deep lines of mistrust.

"We should strike them down now, before their trickery ensnares us all!"

A few of the warriors nodded, their hands tightening on their weapons. Bjorn, ever the pragmatist, remained silent, but his gaze was heavy with unspoken questions. He didn't trust the Zepharians. But neither did he trust the old gods to protect them now. And Bjorn had learned long ago, if the rules changed, so must the warrior.

Erik silenced them all with a single look. His men had followed him across the sea, through blood and fire, through war and famine. They had trusted him to lead them through the storm. They would trust him now. He turned back to the Zepharian, his voice measured, his stance unyielding.

"Show me your knowledge," he commanded, "and I will decide whether you are friend or foe."

The Zepharian raised its hand once more. This time, the light that emanated from its palm did not pulse in a simple glow. It expanded outward, spreading through the air like ink in water, forming shifting symbols of blue fire that hovered in the cold night air.

The warriors gasped, some shielding their faces, others watching in transfixed awe. Before them, an image began to form, a vision so real, so tangible, that Erik could have sworn he was looking through a window into another world.

It was a ship. But not like any Viking longship.

Sleek. Curved. Its form impossibly smooth, without planks, without nails, without sails.

Its hull gleamed like the finest polished steel, but bore symbols—runes of unknown origin—that pulsed with living light. It was beautiful, and yet terrifying.

A ship that needed no wind, no oars. A ship that could defy the waves, defy the very elements themselves. The vision hovered before them, cold and silent, but its presence was deafening.

The warriors stared, their expressions a mixture of awe and terror. The firelight from the longships flickered across their faces, casting them in shadow and flame as they beheld something beyond human comprehension.

Erik inhaled sharply. A thousand thoughts ran through his mind at once, but he could only grasp one.

"It cannot be..." Torvald whispered.

Erik clenched his jaw. But deep inside, beneath the warrior, beneath the conqueror, beneath the blood-soaked king— He knew the truth. The world had changed. And there was no going back.

Chapter 2: The Gift of Knowledge

The air in the fjord was heavy with uncertainty. The Vikings stood in a tight formation, their shields close, weapons clenched in white-knuckled grips. Their breaths formed mist in the freezing night, curling like ghosts between them and the impossible beings before them.

Not a single man spoke. But their eyes, sharp, battle-hardened, moved constantly, watching every flicker of movement, every shadow cast by the silver glow of the visitors who had descended from the sky.

The Zepharians, these strange, otherworldly beings, stood still, their postures unnervingly perfect. Their robes, if they could be called that, rippled with shifting light, like liquid silver flowing over unseen currents.
Their luminescent eyes did not blink, did not shift with unease. They simply watched.

The only sound was the distant lapping of water against the longships, a hollow echo that seemed almost too quiet against the weight of the moment.
The warriors had faced many enemies, men of iron, men of faith, men of kingdoms far beyond their icy shores. But never had they faced something like this.

Erik Bloodaxe's heart pounded beneath his wolf-pelt cloak. His mind was a storm of warring thoughts, clashing like steel upon steel.

These creatures, they stood before him, claiming knowledge beyond the stars. But what did that mean? The Vikings were warriors, not scholars. Their world was one of blood, iron, and the favor of the gods. Their truths were simple: conquer or be conquered, rule or be ruled. What place did these otherworldly visitors have in such a world?

Could knowledge from beyond the sky truly serve a king whose throne was built upon battle and steel? Or was this some elaborate trick? A test from the gods? Or something far worse, a trap laid by deceitful spirits and unseen forces who would seek to unravel the world's order?

He did not trust what he could not see, what he could not fight, what he could not strike down with an axe. But he had seen what these beings could do. And that alone made them dangerous.

He slowly stepped forward, his boots crunching over the frozen earth. His warriors stiffened, shoulders squaring, gripping their weapons tighter. Not out of cowardice, but out of instinct. The instinct that whispered in the bones of every Viking, be ready to fight, be ready to kill, be ready to spill the blood of those who would challenge your dominion.

Torvald's hand twitched over the hilt of his blade; his jaw clenched so tightly that the veins in his neck stood out like cords of iron. He had once served as a goði, a keeper of old rites, long before the axe called him to battle. This—this sorcery from the sky, reeked of trials the gods warned against. Knowledge that came too easily was always laced with ruin.

Gunnar gritted his teeth as he whispered, "This is folly."

He hated how calm Erik looked. As if the world hadn't tilted. As if Gunnar's doubts were just a boy's fear. But he wasn't a boy, not anymore. He'd kill to prove it. To prove he could stand shoulder to shoulder with legends.

Bjorn said nothing, but his fingers flexed against the wood of his axe handle, his expression unreadable beneath the pale light of the aurora. Yet no one interfered. No one stopped Erik from stepping forward.

Because, despite the unnatural power of these visitors, despite the impossible ship that had descended from the sky, despite the voice that had spoken within their very minds, there was one truth that no warrior of the North could ever deny: that Erik Bloodaxe was their king. And if anyone decides the fate of this meeting, it would be him.

Erik stopped just a few paces away from the Zepharian leader, close enough to see the subtle glow of its skin, the way its eyes seemed to reflect the very universe within them. Its features were unreadable, alien yet strangely... calm.

"If you bring knowledge," Erik said at last, his voice steady, strong, unyielding, "then prove it."

For a moment, the Zepharian leader did not move. Then, a flicker of something—was it amusement?—crossed its sharp, inhuman features.

A being that had traveled between the stars, that had seen the rise and fall of civilizations, now looked upon a warrior-king from the cold North with something almost like curiosity. Then, without hesitation, the figure raised its six-fingered hand, palm outward. The Vikings tensed, several of them lifting their shields instinctively. The hum returned, low and resonant, vibrating in their very bones.

The air thickened, the pressure growing heavier, as if the gods themselves had pressed their hands upon the world. The warriors braced themselves, their minds screaming that this was sorcery, witchcraft, a power that no man should wield.

Then, The world changed.

The auroras above flickered and convulsed, their vibrant greens and blues fading into nothingness, devoured by a veil of shifting stars. The fjords, the frozen cliffs, the longships bobbing in the dark waters—all of it dissolved like mist under the morning sun. The air itself changed, thick with something beyond earthly understanding.

Erik's breath caught in his chest. The sky stretched into infinity, no longer bound to the limits of the world he had known. He was no longer in the Northlands. No longer in Midgard. And yet, he still stood, feet firm upon solid ground, though what lay beneath him was no frozen tundra, no rocky shore, no familiar battlefield. It was somewhere else. Somewhere… impossible.

Erik turned his gaze outward and froze. He stood at the edge of an endless battlefield, but it was not like any war he had ever seen. The ground stretched for leagues, not of earth or stone, but something else, smooth, dark as polished obsidian, lined with pulsing veins of blue fire.

Above him, ships of impossible size and design drifted across a sky that was not a sky, their hulls reflecting the cosmic expanse of the universe itself. There were no sails, no oars, yet they moved with power unseen, burning across the void in deadly pursuit of others that glided like predatory birds, sleek and cruel, releasing bursts of pure light that cut through the air like lightning from the gods.

Erik tried to move, to step forward, but the weight of what he was witnessing pressed down upon him like an ocean of stone. This was not a battle of men. It was a war of titans. A war that had raged for longer than he could comprehend. And then, he saw them.

At first, Erik thought they were Vikings, but when he looked closer, his stomach twisted. These warriors were not clad in iron and fur. They wore armor that shimmered like liquid metal, shifting with their movements, reflecting the celestial fires above. Some bore the features of men, faces scarred, battle-worn, their eyes burning with familiar rage. But others—

Others were like the Zepharians, their forms taller, more elongated, their features too perfect, too alien, yet twisted with a battle fury that was unmistakably human. They clashed with weapons unlike anything Erik had ever seen.

Blades that hummed with power, axes that burned with living fire, spears that crackled with raw energy, each strike sending shockwaves through the battlefield.
He saw men crushed beneath the weight of enemies they could not understand. He saw warriors rise again, reforged in a fire that was not of this world. And yet—
Something about it felt familiar. As if he had seen this before. As if it was already written in his bones, in his fate, in the runes of time itself.

Then, he saw himself.

Not as he was now. But transformed. His armor gleamed like the night sky, the runes along his arms burning with an energy that pulsed in time with his heartbeat. And in his hands he carried a great axe. Not forged of steel, but of something brighter, something alive, its edge shimmering with a light that did not belong to this world.

His breath caught, his body tensed as he watched himself stride forward, leading warriors who had become more than men. Vikings who wielded powers beyond mortal comprehension, their roars shaking the very heavens, their steps cracking the battlefield beneath them. They charged into the maelstrom, their weapons tearing through the enemy, their spirits unbroken despite the horrors that awaited them. And then—The shadow appeared.

At first, it was just a distant shape, a ripple in the void.
But as Erik's eyes focused, his blood turned to ice.
A black mass, writhing, growing, consuming the stars themselves. It moved not as a beast, not as a god.

But as a hunger given form. It devoured everything in its path, not just flesh and steel, not just ships and warriors—but light itself. And it was coming. For them. For everything.

A voice rumbled through his mind, deep and ancient, its words vibrating through his bones, through his soul.

"The Svarthjarta… the Black Heart… It comes for all things."

Erik staggered back, his breath ragged. His hands trembled. Not with fear. But with something deeper. A sense of fate tightening its grip upon him.

The visions blinked away, vanishing like mist before the rising sun. Suddenly, he was back in the fjord, his boots planted firmly upon the frozen earth, the cold wind howling through the cliffs once more. His warriors surrounded him, their expressions a mix of concern and confusion.

The Zepharians stood motionless, their silver eyes reflecting the fading glow of the auroras above. The world had returned. And yet, Erik knew that nothing would ever be the same again. The wind hit him like a hammer, biting through his furs, but he hardly felt it.

Torvald, still clutching his sword, took an uneasy step forward.

"Erik… what did you see?"

The question hung in the frozen air, heavy with unspoken dread. Erik's fingers twitched, his mind still reeling from the weight of what had been revealed. Slowly, he turned his gaze toward the Zepharian leader, his voice hoarse but steady.

"What was that?"

The Zepharian inclined its head, the silver glow in its eyes shifting slightly.

"Your future."

It let the words linger.

"Or a path it may take."

Erik thought, if that was the future... was it his fate or his failure? Had the gods sent these beings, or had they abandoned him? And if so, what was he, without their favor?

A murmur rippled through the Vikings, low and uneasy, like the first tremors before an avalanche. Some warriors muttered prayers, invoking Odin, Thor, and Freyja, their lips moving in whispers meant to ward off ill omens. Others tightened their grips on their weapons, exchanging wary glances with their king, their gazes flickering between Erik and the beings that had stepped from the stars.

The air was heavy, not with frost, not with the weight of battle, but with something else entirely, the burden of what had been revealed, the weight of what was yet to come. Gunnar, still clutching the hilt of his blade, suddenly spat onto the frozen ground, the sharp crack of saliva against ice breaking the silence.

"And why should we believe these visions?" he demanded. His voice was sharp, defiant. "What trickery is this?"

His eyes burned with the fire of a warrior who had been taught that power was won through steel and blood, not given through whispers and light.

The Zepharian leader did not react to the insult, its expression unchanged, unreadable, as though it had long since moved beyond the concerns of mortal men. Instead, it took a slow, deliberate step forward, its movement so fluid it was almost unnatural, bringing itself closer to Erik.

The warriors shifted uneasily, fingers tightening around axe handles, shoulders bracing, every muscle ready to strike if needed. But Erik stood his ground. And the Zepharian spoke.

"Because the future is already set in motion."

Its voice, though not spoken, resonated through the air, felt rather than heard.

"And without knowledge, you will be swept away by it, like a reed in a storm."

Erik's pulse still thundered, but his voice was steady now.

"What knowledge?" he demanded.

The warriors fell silent, waiting for the answer.

"You claim to offer wisdom from the stars," Erik continued, his blue eyes locked onto the silver gaze of the being before him. "But we are Vikings. We do not seek knowledge for its own sake. We take, we conquer. We do not beg for wisdom like helpless children."

At that, the Zepharian's silver eyes flickered, a strange gleam within them—not anger, not insult, but something else entirely.

"And that," the Zepharian said, "is why you intrigue us."

The words sent another shiver through the warriors, for they carried a weight that none of them fully understood.

A second Zepharian stepped forward, its robe shifting like flowing mercury, its form almost weightless, unbound by the very world around it. It raised a hand, palm open, and the earth itself responded.

The warriors staggered back, some muttering curses, others gripping their shields as if facing an unseen enemy. Something began to take shape from the frozen ground, not in the air, not as a vision, but from the very fabric of reality itself. A longship. But not like any Viking ship Erik had ever seen.

Its hull was not wood, nor bound with iron rivets. It was sleek, curved, dark as the void itself, its surface not carved, but forged from something ancient, something that did not belong to this world. Instead of oars, lines of pulsing blue runes ran along the ship's hull, glowing with a power that neither fire nor storm could produce. It breathed, almost as if it was alive.

The warriors stared, wide-eyed, some with expressions of awe, others with pure terror. Torvald's face twisted in disgust.

"It is unnatural," he muttered. His voice was low, yet filled with warning, like a man who had glimpsed something forbidden. "The gods did not craft this."

Erik did not look at him. Instead, he stepped closer to the vessel, his gloved fingers brushing its surface.
It was cold, but not like steel. It thrummed beneath his touch, humming softly, almost as if it was... waiting.

The Zepharian leader spoke again.

"This," it said, "is knowledge. A gift. A means for your people to become greater than they are."

The words hung in the air, carrying a weight greater than steel, greater than kingship, greater than any war Erik had ever fought.

The warriors hesitated behind him, waiting for their king's reaction. Bjorn Stonehand, the most seasoned among them, finally broke the silence.

"A gift? Or a curse?"

His voice was grim, his eyes never leaving the strange ship. Erik's fingers tightened against the hull of the vessel.

"The gods did not craft the longship either," he said softly.

A silence followed. Not of fear, but of realization. The Vikings had always embraced the unknown and had sailed beyond the horizon, defying death itself in pursuit of new lands, new plunder, and new conquest. Perhaps this was no different. Perhaps this was the next great horizon. He turned back toward the Zepharians, his stance firm.

"And if I refuse?"

The Zepharian leader's silver gaze hardened for the first time, its expression turning from passive observation to something more... absolute.

"Then you will perish," it said. "As all others who refuse knowledge have perished."

The words cut through the frozen air like a blade, sharp as steel, cold as the North wind. The warriors shifted uneasily, and the unspoken meaning of the words settled upon them like a burial shroud. Erik exhaled. He knew, in that moment, there was no turning back. The choice had already been made. Even if he did not yet understand it.

Chapter 3: The Viking Age

The Drakenskip loomed before them, its dark, curved hull shimmering beneath the shifting lights of the aurora-lit sky. It was like nothing the Vikings had ever laid eyes upon—a thing of impossible craftsmanship, its smooth surface pulsing with an eerie, living glow, as though the runes carved into its body breathed.

The warriors stood frozen, staring at the vessel before them, their minds struggling to grasp its presence in their world. For all their years of raiding, sailing, and conquest, they had known many ships, longships that cut through the waves with the grace of a hunting wolf, merchant vessels that carried the spoils of war, warships that bore them to battle against kings and emperors. But nothing in their world had ever looked like this.

Torvald, took a slow step forward, his boots crunching against the frost-covered ground. He had seen cursed relics before, monstrous things left by those who worshipped false gods. This ship felt the same. Too smooth. Too silent. It reeked of things man was not meant to touch.

"This... this is no longship."

His voice was hoarse, edged with something he would never dare name fear. Gunnar, younger and more reckless, narrowed his sharp, battle-hardened eyes.

"It bears no oars, no mast. How does it move?"

His fingers twitched against the handle of his axe, as if he expected the ship to awaken, to strike out like a beast. The Zepharian leader did not answer immediately. Instead, it turned its luminous silver gaze toward Erik, as though it had only ever intended to speak to him.

"It moves because it must."

The voice did not come from its lips, yet Erik heard it clearly, reverberating in his very bones.

"And it will take you where no longship has ever gone before."

The words settled like an omen, whispering through the warriors like a bitter wind.

The silence stretched between them, thick as the deepest fog. The wind howled, swirling tiny ice crystals through the air, making the world feel smaller, contained within this one moment.

The warriors exchanged uneasy glances, their hands drifting toward their weapons, as though steel alone could guard them against the unknown. But steel could not fight what they faced now. This was not a battle of flesh and blood. This was a battle of fate.

And Erik Bloodaxe stood at the threshold of something greater than himself. He exhaled a slow, deliberate breath, his chest rising and falling beneath his wolf-pelt cloak. The Zepharians were powerful; that much was certain. But they had not come as conquerors. They had not raised weapons, not demanded tribute, not spoken in threats. They had offered something else entirely. Knowledge. And Erik knew, knowledge was the sharpest blade of all.

"You wish to give us this... ship?" Erik asked, his voice steady, despite the uncertainty pressing at the edges of his mind.

The Zepharian leader inclined its head, its silver eyes flashing with something unreadable.

"We offer a choice."

It gestured toward the Drakenskip, the runes along its hull pulsing in perfect harmony with the breath of the wind.

"Take the Drakenskip, and your people will ascend."

The light flickered across its metallic robes, shifting like liquid silver in the firelight.

"Reject it, and history will consume you."

Erik studied the strange vessel before him. Slowly, he extended his gloved hand, his fingers brushing against its sleek, unnatural surface. And beneath his touch, the runes pulsed. Alive. There was something inside this ship, something waiting, watching, breathing.

His mind raced. Could this ship give them dominion over the seas? Could they become gods among men, ruling the world with a force no other kingdom could match? Or was this a test or a lure to turn them away from the gods of their ancestors?

Behind him, his warriors stirred, their faces a mixture of awe and dread. Some looked eager, already dreaming of the power this ship could bring. Others looked fearful, as though they had already seen their doom written in its glowing runes.

Gunnar stepped forward, eyes wide, a child before a bonfire.

"With this ship, we could cross the oceans in a day. No kingdom could stand against us."

He didn't see magic, he saw destiny.

Torvald, ever cautious, took another step forward, his voice barely above a whisper.

"You do not trust them, do you?"

Bjorn whispered to himself quietly.

"The gods gave us oars once. Then sails. Maybe now they give us this."

He didn't fear the ship. He feared what they'd become without it.

Erik did not look away from the ship.

"I trust only in power."

The words were cold, final, like the strike of an axe on flesh. And this ship, whatever it was, held power beyond measure.

Erik turned, his sharp blue eyes scanning the faces of his men, warriors who had sailed with him through storms and slaughter, who had followed him into fire and blood. And now they waited for his command. His choice. He lifted his chin, his voice clear as the winter wind.

"We will take it."

His ancestors would call it blasphemy. His enemies would call it madness. But Erik saw something else in the ship's pale glow, a future that feared no winter. No spear. No god.

The words rang through the fjord, sinking into the bones of every man who heard them. A ripple of shock and awe passed through the warriors. Some nodded in approval, their expressions hardened with determination. Others muttered prayers to Odin and Thor, unsure if they had just witnessed the first step toward ascension or doom.

The Zepharians did not smile, nor did they speak of gratitude. They simply turned toward the Drakenskip, their

movements precise and smooth, as though this had already
been decided long before Erik spoke the words aloud. A low
hum filled the air, and the ship's core came alive. A pulse of
blue light radiated outward, spreading in circular patterns
across the hull, illuminating the fjord with an unearthly
glow. The ground trembled beneath their feet. The air
thickened, pressing down upon them like the weight of an
unseen force. And then, the world shuddered. Like the first
breath of a new dawn, the ship exhaled, and the Viking Age
changed forever.

The First Voyage

The warriors gathered on the deck of the Drakenskip, their
boots clanking uneasily against the smooth metal surface.
The ship was massive, larger than any longship they had
ever seen, and yet it had no oars, no sails, no rudder. Its
blackened hull pulsed with soft blue light, runes etched in
patterns that no mortal craftsman could have carved,
glowing like embers waiting to ignite.
It felt alive. And that unsettled them.

Torvald ran a calloused hand along the hull, his fingers
twitching slightly at the strange hum beneath his palm.

"How does it move?" he muttered, his voice edged with
suspicion.

It was unnatural. A ship that did not answer to the wind or
the tides. A ship that felt as though it had been forged from
the bones of gods and demons alike.

The Zepharian leader remained silent for a moment,
studying them as one might observe a flame flickering
against the night sky. Then, with that same unnerving
stillness, it spoke.

"You will see soon enough."

The words carried an undeniable weight, like an unspoken promise. The warriors exchanged glances, their hands never straying too far from their weapons. Even in the face of the unknown, a Viking's grip never faltered on the hilt of his sword.

At the helm, Erik Bloodaxe stood, his breath slow, deliberate. In his hands, he gripped a control unlike anything he had ever known. It was not a wheel, not a tiller, not rope nor oar, but something greater, something deeper. A pedestal pulsed beneath his fingers, its surface warm, as though it possessed a life of its own.

"It feels... alive," Erik muttered under his breath.

Then, without warning, the ship moved. Not by wind. Not by the pull of the tides. Not by any force Erik had ever commanded before. It simply rose.

The warriors staggered back, their eyes widening as the Drakenskip lifted itself from the water, defying every law they had ever known. Gasps of awe and terror erupted from the crew. Some clutched their weapons as though readying for battle. Others fell to their knees, their voices muttering prayers to Odin, to Thor, to whatever god might listen. Torvald's breath hitched.

"By Odin's beard—"

Higher. Higher. The fjord shrank beneath them, the jagged cliffs growing smaller, the great sea becoming nothing but a black mirror far below. Some warriors dropped to their knees, whispering last rites. Others laughed, half madness, half ecstasy. Even the stars above seemed to pause, watching the sons of Midgard leave the cradle of their gods. And then—

The stars exploded into view. A sky not meant for mortal men stretched endlessly before them. The Drakenskip had left the world of men.

Beyond the Sky

Erik's breath came short, his chest tightening.
For all his years of war and conquest, he had never felt fear like this. The air around them shifted, not cold, not warm—something else entirely. A void that swallowed sound, a silence deeper than anything he had ever known.

His warriors gripped their weapons, knuckles white, but what good was a blade in a world without wind or stone or sea? Gunnar's voice came as a whisper, barely audible.

"This is not right."

His hands trembled against his sword.

"Men were not meant to leave the sea."
Erik exhaled slowly, his eyes never leaving the abyss beyond the ship's hull.

"And yet here we are."

Through the glass-like panels along the ship's sides, they could see the world beneath them—a vast sphere of ice and ocean, floating in an endless black abyss.

The warriors stared in stunned silence, the weight of what they were seeing crushing them like a warhammer to the chest.

"The world is small," Torvald murmured.

He had sailed across many seas, fought battles in distant lands, but now, he saw the truth. Everything they had known—the wars, the kingdoms, the gods—was nothing but a speck in the great void beyond the sky.
Erik said nothing. He could not look away. This was power. This was dominion. And it was only the beginning.

The Great Return

The journey back to the world of men was as silent as the void they had passed through. The warriors did not speak, their minds still trying to grasp the impossible.

And then— The Drakenskip descended, returning them to the frozen earth. The Vikings disembarked as changed men. Their eyes had seen what no warrior had ever witnessed. They had sailed beyond the reach of the sea, beyond the limits of their gods. They had looked into the abyss, and the abyss had looked back at them. The seas were no longer their limit. The stars called to them.

The Next Step

Erik turned to the Zepharian leader, his mind still racing, his thoughts a storm of war, of conquest, of what was to come.

"What now?" he asked.

The Zepharian watched him, and for the first time since their arrival, its lips curved into something resembling a smile.

"Now," it said, "you will learn how to wield what you have been given."

Chapter 4: Disappearance

Years had passed since Erik Bloodaxe and his warriors first sailed beyond the world of men, touching the stars themselves. The old ways remained, but something had changed within them. They had once been raiders, conquerors, wolves upon the waves, feared by kings and emperors alike. But now, they had become something more. Their axes had tasted the blood of men, their ships had conquered the seas. Now, they set their sights upon the stars themselves. And then, One day, they were gone.

There had been no war, no disease, no great disaster to explain their disappearance. No plague swept through their strongholds, no foreign invader came to claim their lands. Yet the fjords of Norway, once alive with the sound of warriors preparing for battle, the laughter of feasting clans, the ringing of hammers upon steel, had fallen silent.

The longships that had once filled the harbors, their dragon-headed prows cutting through the ice-laced waters like wolves hunting prey, were gone. The great halls of Erik's kingdom, where kings and warriors had gathered to drink, to boast, to sing the songs of their victories, stood empty. Their fires had long since died, reduced to nothing more than cold ash. The fishing villages along the coastline, once teeming with life, had been abandoned, their homes left as though their inhabitants had simply stood up and walked away, never to return. The mountains bore no echo of smiths at work, no distant shouts of training warriors. The great shields that once lined the long halls, once symbols of strength and unity, now hung motionless, untouched by hands that would never return.

And no one knew why. No bodies were found. No graves were dug. It was as if the entire Viking people had simply stepped out of history itself. They had vanished.

Some said they heard horns in the wind for years after. That the stars above the fjords burned just a little brighter. That the gods had not taken them... but something older had Not slain in battle. Not conquered by an enemy. Simply... Gone.

Legends whispered of the last night the Norsemen walked the earth. Some spoke of strange lights in the sky, a storm of fire and shadow that descended upon the fjords. Others claimed to have heard the thunder of war drums, though no enemy had come to their shores.

An old fisherman, the last man to see Erik's stronghold before it fell silent, told a tale that had been passed down through the centuries.

"I saw them, standing upon the cliffs, staring at the sky," he had said.

"They were not afraid. They did not run. They simply waited."

"Then the heavens split apart, and they were gone."

But as time passed, even these stories faded. They became myths, fairy tales, nothing more than the ramblings of old men with too much mead in their bellies. The world moved on. And the Vikings faded from history.

The year was 2045. The world had long since moved past the age of the Viking warriors. The once-mighty Norsemen were but a footnote in history books, their legacy preserved only in museum exhibits and half-remembered legends. Empires had risen and fallen.

Wars had redrawn borders a hundred times over.

Technology had replaced steel and fire, and humanity had conquered the skies with machines. And yet—one mystery remained unsolved.

The disappearance of Erik Bloodaxe and his people. Historians had searched the fjords, had dug through ruins, had pored over ancient texts, and yet no explanation had ever been found. It was a puzzle that had haunted scholars for centuries. And then— One woman found the first clue.

Dr. Astrid Jorgensen was not a woman who believed in myths. She was a historian, an archaeologist, a seeker of truth in the bones of the past. Her work had taken her across the world, from the tombs of ancient kings to lost civilizations buried beneath the sands of time. She had debunked legends, had proven the falsehoods of countless tales, and had spent her career separating fantasy from reality. And yet, Something about the disappearance of the Vikings had always troubled her.

It was not like the fall of Rome, not like the collapse of forgotten empires. They had not faded through war, nor had they been wiped out by famine or plague. They had simply vanished. And there were no records, no explanations, nothing but silence.

She had grown up hearing sagas from her grandmother, stories told in a dialect older than the capital's streets. She'd dismissed them, until the runes started to feel like memories.

For years, she had sought answers. And then, while researching ancient Nordic ruins along the Norwegian coastline, she found it. A stone, buried beneath centuries of earth, carved with runes that did not belong to any known Viking script. Runes that glowed faintly, as though whispering to those who dared look upon them.

Runes that did not belong to the world of men.
She ran her fingers over the markings, her heart pounding.

The inscription was clear, precise, though the language was older than any she had ever studied. And at the very bottom, etched in symbols not of this world, was a single phrase she could understand.

"The Black Heart Comes."

Her breath hitched. Her hands trembled. And in that moment, she knew that the Vikings had not vanished. They had been taken.

The Arctic wind howled through the desolate remains of the Viking stronghold, sweeping across the snow-covered ruins like the whispers of long-dead warriors.

Dr. Astrid Jorgensen pulled her coat tighter around her shoulders, the bitter cold cutting through even the thickest layers of fabric. Her breath formed misty clouds in the freezing air as she surveyed the excavation site—a stretch of ice-covered land that had once been a thriving Viking settlement. But what lay beneath the ice was what truly mattered.

"Dr. Jorgensen!" a voice called through the radio.

She pressed a gloved hand to her earpiece. "What is it?"

"You... you need to see this."

Heart pounding, Astrid rushed toward the dig site, her boots crunching against the ice. Her research team had been working for months, trying to uncover the truth about the sudden disappearance of Erik Bloodaxe's people.

They had expected old artifacts, perhaps weapons or ship fragments. What they found instead defied everything. Buried deep beneath the ice—a ship. But not just any ship.

It was not wood, nor iron. It was sleek, black metal, smooth as glass, pulsing faintly beneath the frost. Strange runes lined its surface, symbols that bore a striking resemblance to Viking carvings—yet were unmistakably... alien.

Astrid's breath caught.

"My God..." she whispered.

The discovery spread like wildfire. What began as a routine excavation turned into the most significant archaeological event of the century. Within hours, the site was flooded with historians, scientists, and military officials, each desperate to understand what had been uncovered. By nightfall, satellite scans had been rerouted from classified government projects, redirected to Norway's frozen wastelands, their data pouring into the hands of specialists who had spent their lives searching for proof of lost civilizations. But no one had expected this.

The first images were relayed from drones scanning deep beneath the surface. At first, the scientists thought it was a mistake, some kind of false reading caused by the ice shifting over the centuries. But then— The outlines became clearer.

What they saw stopped the entire excavation in its tracks. There, frozen beneath layers of ancient ice, were ships. Not wooden longships, not the remnants of Norse settlements, but something far older. Something impossible. An entire fleet lay preserved in the ice, untouched by time.
Their alien metal hulls shimmered beneath the permafrost, their sleek forms perfectly intact despite having been buried for over a thousand years. The scientists could not explain it.

The historians had no words for it. And the military officers who had arrived to observe the dig knew only one thing—

This discovery changed everything.

"How is this possible?" one researcher asked, his voice hushed, almost reverent, as though afraid of the answer.

"These ships… they predate any known technological advancement by over a thousand years."

The room fell silent, the weight of the discovery pressing down on them like a tombstone on history itself. Dr. Astrid Jorgensen stood motionless, her fingertips tracing the strange runes etched into one of the exposed surfaces. The symbols were both familiar and foreign, carved with the precision of a Viking craftsman, yet bearing the unmistakable marks of something beyond human hands. Her breath hitched.

"These symbols… they are both Viking and something else entirely."

Her voice was barely above a whisper, but every eye in the room turned toward her.

"If Erik Bloodaxe's people disappeared… did they truly vanish?"

The question hung in the air, unspoken fears creeping into the minds of everyone present. A heavy silence filled the research tent.

Then, the radio crackled.

"Dr. Jorgensen, we… we found something inside."

The first human remains were discovered inside one of the uncovered ships. Unlike anything the team had ever seen. The body, though frozen, was perfectly preserved—trapped in ice as though time itself had paused around him.

The scientists gathered around in stunned silence, their breath fogging in the cold air as they stared at the warrior before them. A Viking. But not one that belonged to any history book. His armor was unmistakably Norse, bearing the sigils of warriors long since lost to time, yet... it had been altered. Modified in ways that defied explanation. His breastplate shimmered unnaturally, the metal pulsing faintly, as though charged with a power that had not yet faded. His helmet bore symbols not of Norse origin, patterns that shifted under the light, reacting as though they were alive. And even his bones appeared denser, different, as though they had been changed by something beyond human understanding.

Astrid knelt beside the body, her fingers trembling as she brushed away the last of the frost that clung to his hands. Her stomach twisted. There, beneath the frozen skin— Runes. Not carved. Not tattooed. But woven into the very flesh itself. They pulsed beneath the ice, as though still holding onto the remnants of some forgotten power.

Astrid exhaled sharply, her voice barely audible.

"This isn't possible."

The researchers behind her shifted uneasily, watching in muted horror.

"This man... he should not exist."

One of the researchers crossed himself. Another whispered a prayer in Old Norse. No one spoke of it, but every person in the room knew that they hadn't found a corpse. They had found a warning.

And yet, he did. The implications were world-shattering.

But even before the sun set, satellite feeds began to stutter. Data vanished from servers. And black vans with no insignia arrived before the press could set up their tripods.

The world had changed. But those in power would never let the truth surface so easily. Within two days, the excavation was shut down. Government forces arrived under the cover of night, moving with the efficiency of men who had done this before.

The site was sealed off, soldiers replacing the scientists and researchers who had spent their lives unearthing the past. Dr. Astrid Jorgensen and her team were removed, their access denied, their research confiscated before they could even fully comprehend what they had found.

Astrid herself was taken, escorted away under the highest levels of global security clearance. She was interrogated for hours, pressed for every detail of what she had uncovered.

And then, she was instructed to keep silent. But no matter what they told her, no matter the threats, the orders, the denials, she knew what she had seen. And she knew this was only the beginning. Because the Vikings had not simply vanished, they had been taken. They had changed. And somewhere, out there, beyond the stars, the descendants of Erik Bloodaxe's lost warriors were waiting. And soon, the world would remember them.

They could bury the ships. Seal the site. Silence her voice. But Astrid had seen too much. And now, she carried the flame.

Chapter 5: Return of the Zepharians

The world was not ready for what was about to happen. For centuries, the legend of Erik Bloodaxe's disappearance had remained just that, a legend, a tale told by scholars and skalds alike.

Even after Dr. Astrid Jorgensen's discovery of the Viking fleet buried beneath the Arctic ice, ships made of impossible metal, their hulls pulsing with forgotten energy, the truth had been locked away.

Governments had moved swiftly, sweeping the discovery under layers of secrecy, deeming the implications too dangerous for the public to know. But secrets cannot stay buried forever. And on a cold winter night in Norway, the Zepharians returned.

The first signs were subtle, easily dismissed by those who refused to see the truth. It began with unusual aurora activity, waves of green and blue light flickering across the sky in patterns that seemed too precise, too deliberate. At first, scientists dismissed the disturbance.

"A fluctuation in the Earth's magnetic field," they claimed.

But the lights didn't behave like any aurora they had seen before. They twisted and spiraled, forming patterns, intricate symbols that seemed to shift and dance across the heavens.

Days later, the power grids across Scandinavia failed simultaneously, plunging cities into darkness without warning. In Oslo, emergency services battled frozen streets and panicked citizens, while Tromsø's skies seemed to blaze with impossible fire.

Children cried in their sleep, dreaming of fire and ice. Dogs refused to go outside. In the silence between blackouts, an old woman in Tromsø whispered an old Viking prayer, one that hadn't been spoken aloud in a hundred winters.

Reports flooded in from Iceland, Sweden, and Denmark, their communications failing, compasses spinning wildly, ships losing their course on calm seas.

It was as though the Earth itself had grown restless, its rhythms disturbed by a presence that had not yet revealed itself. Then came the lights.

It began as orbs of silver, faint and distant, drifting low through the clouds, silent and cold. Then they grew larger, brighter, until their glow was blinding, washing the snow-covered fields of Norway in pale silver light. The orbs descended, moving without sound, ignoring the laws of wind and gravity. They hovered above mountaintops, valleys, and fjords, defying everything humanity understood about the natural world.
And then—

The Zepharians returned. For the first time in a thousand years, they walked the Earth once more.

At exactly 2:14 AM, the first Zepharian ships touched down just outside Tromsø, Norway, their metallic hulls shimmering beneath the moonlit sky. Military response teams were already on high alert. Within minutes, helicopters circled the landing zones, their rotors cutting through the frozen air.

Armored vehicles rumbled across the icy roads, their treads crushing the frost-covered earth as soldiers in black combat gear formed defensive barricades around the alien vessels. Spotlights illuminated the ships' smooth, seamless surfaces, casting long shadows across the frozen fields.

Inside a secured government facility, Dr. Astrid Jorgensen stood before a wall of monitors, watching the unfolding events with a sense of dread and awe. She didn't panic. She watched. Measured. These weren't gods. They were tacticians,just like she was. And she needed to know their game before anyone else did.

She had spent years chasing the truth, only to have it revealed to the world in a way that no one could control. Her pulse quickened as she saw the hull of one ship split open, a seam forming in the metal as though it were peeling itself apart.

The crowd of soldiers tensed, rifles raised. And then they stepped out.

Tall, silver-skinned figures emerged from the ship, their metallic robes rippling like liquid mercury with each deliberate step. Their eyes—pale silver orbs without pupils—glowed faintly, casting a dim shimmer across their faces.

They moved with an unnatural precision, each step perfectly measured, each motion fluid and precise, as though they flowed through the air rather than walking upon the earth. They were exactly as they had been described in Viking lore—tall, graceful, and inhumanly perfect. And yet... Something was different. Their presence was no longer that of observers. This time, they had come with purpose.

The soldiers held their ground, their eyes flicking between the towering figures and their commanders. The Zepharians showed no aggression, no hint of hostility. They merely stood in silent formation, watching the soldiers with expressions that seemed neither curious nor cold, just... patient.

It was not the silence of peace. It was the silence of a blade before it falls. They were not asking for permission. They were waiting for the reckoning to begin.

Ingrid's heart hammered in her chest.

"What are they waiting for?" she whispered.

Then, one of the Zepharians, taller than the rest, its robe
pulsing faintly with threads of violet energy, stepped
forward. It raised a six-fingered hand, fingers spread wide,
palm outward. A pulse of energy rippled outward, sweeping
over the soldiers like a winter wind.

It wasn't violent, there was no shockwave, no force.
But every human present felt it, a vibration deep in their
bones, like the tolling of a distant bell that refused to stop.

The air seemed to thicken, heavy with something old and
powerful. And then, the Zepharian's voice echoed through
their minds.

"We return for the sons and daughters of the North."

Ingrid's breath caught.

"The sons and daughters of the North..." she whispered.

The meaning was clear. The Zepharians had not come to
conquer. They had come to reclaim.

The Zepharian leader, standing taller than any human, took
a deliberate step forward. Its form seemed to blur and
ripple, as if the air itself strained to contain its presence. Its
eyes glowed silver, like molten metal swirling inside a glass
sphere.

The crowd of soldiers, scientists, and leaders stood frozen,
their breath visible in the frozen night air. No translator was
required. The Zepharian's voice entered their minds,
bypassing language barriers, speaking in a tone that
resonated in their very bones.

"You have found what was buried. The time of waiting is over."

The words were not just heard, they were felt. Each syllable vibrated like a hammer striking iron, ringing through minds and memories alike. A hush fell over the gathered military forces, the usual barked orders and murmured whispers silenced by something far greater.

The Zepharian's gaze swept across the crowd, pausing on faces marked with fear, confusion, and anger. Then it spoke again:

"Erik Bloodaxe's people were not lost. "They left to prepare. Now, they are returning."

The words fell like stones dropped in still water, rippling outward with unsettling force. The world seemed to shudder beneath their weight.

The silence that followed was thick and oppressive. For years, the legend of Erik Bloodaxe's disappearance had been dismissed as myth, a fading tale of warriors lost to time. But this... this changed everything.

"Erik's people... they left?" a soldier murmured, barely able to voice the thought.

"If they left..." another whispered, "where did they go?"

More importantly, Why were they returning now? Questions swirled like storm winds, but no answer came. The Zepharians stood motionless, revealing nothing more. And that terrified people more than any threat ever could.

The Zepharians' arrival set the world into chaos. In the weeks that followed, entire nations splintered under the pressure of uncertainty. Some leaders welcomed the Zepharians, believing they heralded an era of advancement, knowledge, and power.

"They bring us strength," one Scandinavian prime minister declared. "We must embrace the change they offer."

Others saw the Zepharians as a threat, claiming they had come to conquer, to manipulate mankind. Protests erupted in the streets of Berlin, London, and New York, citizens chanting for their governments to strike first before the Zepharians could act.

Religious leaders warned that the Zepharians were false gods, agents of deception sent to lure humanity from its path. Meanwhile, secret organizations, long aware of the Zepharian presence, emerged from the shadows. They had known the truth for decades, that Erik Bloodaxe's disappearance had never been a mystery.

For centuries, they had guarded the evidence, suppressing knowledge of the Drakenskip and the strange technology it carried. But now, those secrets had been dragged into the light. The world was no longer divided by nations, but by fear and belief. And as world leaders debated their response, the true storm was already coming.

On the third night after the landing, something changed. Deep within a military command center, scientists and intelligence officers monitored the skies. Radio towers, satellites, and deep-space scanners were trained on the edges of the galaxy, tracking anything that might reveal the Zepharians' intentions. And then, the signal came.

It began as a low pulse, barely audible. At first, they thought it was static, an error in their equipment. But as the pulses continued, the pattern became clearer, rhythmic transmission, pulsing like the heartbeat of something ancient. It was not Zepharian in origin. It was older. It was darker.

Astrid Jorgensen was among the scientists monitoring the incoming data, her fingers trembling as she traced the rhythm of the signal.

"This... this isn't theirs," she murmured, her breath clouding the chilled air.

The room seemed colder, the very walls pressing inward with an unnatural presence.

"What is it?" Astrid asked aloud, more to herself than anyone else.

The answer came not from a human, but from the Zepharian leader. It turned toward her, its gaze sharper than before. Its silver eyes darkened, like a sky swallowing its stars.

"It is what Erik Bloodaxe feared."

Ingrid's heart lurched. The room fell silent.

"It is what comes for us all. It is not a beast. It is not a mind. It is hunger made manifest. A void with memory. And now... it remembers us."

The Zepharian's gaze seemed to burn through Ingrid, as if the truth were searing itself directly into her mind.

"The Svarthjarta."

The room seemed to dim, as though even the lights feared the word.

"The Black Heart."

Astrid swallowed hard.

"What... what does it want?"

The Zepharian's voice was cold, heavy, and carried no emotion.

"It wants to consume."

"It devours light. It devours life. It devours worlds."

The Zepharian's ships, which had remained still since their arrival, lifted from the earth, their sleek hulls rising into the sky.

They formed defensive formations, each vessel glowing with a dim pulse of violet energy.

"They're retreating," a scientist whispered in awe.

"No," Astrid said softly, her face pale.

"They're preparing."

In the sky above Norway, the auroras writhed violently, twisting like serpents of green and violet flame. Somewhere, out there, The Svarthjarta was coming. And the world's only hope now rested with the descendants of Erik Bloodaxe's forgotten warriors. The Zepharians had returned with a purpose. And time was running out.

The gods had not forsaken Earth. They had simply been outpaced. And now, the last hope lay not in prayers... but in blood, memory, and steel.

Chapter 6: The Descendants

The world was changing. Since the Zepharians' return, the veil of mystery that had once shrouded the fate of Erik Bloodaxe and his warriors had been lifted. The truth, once buried beneath centuries of myth and legend, was now undeniable.

Erik's people had not vanished into myth, nor had war or plague wiped them from the Earth. They had left. They had sailed beyond the world of men, forging their path among the stars, preparing for something far greater than any war humanity had ever imagined.

And now… They were coming back. But not in the way anyone had expected.

The first signs appeared just days after the Zepharians delivered their cryptic warning. It began with dreams, vivid, impossible visions that seemed to bleed into reality. Men and women across Scandinavia, Iceland, and Greenland awoke in the night, drenched in sweat, their minds filled with images they could barely comprehend. They saw battlefields beyond the stars, places that stretched far beyond the limits of Earthly understanding.

Mountains of black stone loomed under blood-red skies, and alien war machines clashed in the distance—blades forged of light and flame, cutting through warriors clad in metal and energy. The visions were detailed, too much so to be dismissed as imagination. Many saw strange banners flying on those battlefields, banners adorned with Nordic runes, bearing the sigils of clans long forgotten.

Some heard the roar of Vikings, their voices calling out in a tongue older than time itself. Some even claimed to see Erik Bloodaxe himself, his mighty axe raised high, leading a war host composed of warriors unlike anything Earth had ever known.

And then came the physical changes. At first, they were subtle: a sharper mind, faster reflexes, a heightened awareness of the world. But soon the changes grew… more pronounced.

Men who had been frail found themselves lifting weights they could never have managed before. Women who had struggled with poor eyesight began to see with unnatural clarity, able to read distant carvings or spot distant figures moving on the horizon. Others felt their hearing sharpen, able to pick out whispers from across crowded streets. It was more than just strength and awareness—it was something deeper. They were changing, becoming something else.

And then came the memories. They started as flashes, fleeting moments that flickered behind the eyes like the afterglow of lightning. A warrior standing on a burning battlefield, axe in hand. A ship sailing through blackened space, its glowing runes blazing like embers against the void. The face of a king, armored in gleaming plates forged from metals no Earthly forge had ever crafted. The memories were not their own, yet they felt as real as any lived experience.

She had been a linguist in Berlin. Fluent in seven Earth languages. But now she spoke a dialect no one could identify, because it hadn't been spoken in ten thousand years. She wept when she heard her own voice. It didn't sound like hers anymore

Those afflicted could remember details that no mortal should know, the names of fallen comrades, the taste of air from a world that existed light-years away, the feeling of steel meeting flesh as they fought on alien soil. It became clear that these were not dreams.

These were ancestral memories, fragments passed down through blood and bone, stored in their very genetic code—waiting to be awakened. By the time the world's scientists began investigating, the pattern had become clear. Those experiencing the dreams, the visions, and the transformations were all descendants of the lost Norse warriors.

Fishermen from the frozen coastline of Norway, soldiers stationed in Iceland, descendants of Viking settlers in Greenland—they had all been touched by the awakening. It was as if some ancient trigger, buried within their DNA, had been activated. A forgotten piece of their ancestral past had resurfaced, breathing life into abilities that had long lain dormant.

But these gifts came with a weight, a sense of dread, of urgency. Those who felt the change knew, instinctively, that they had not been awakened for no reason.

The Svarthjarta was coming. The Black Heart, a force that devoured worlds, that consumed light itself, had found them. The forgotten warriors of Erik Bloodaxe's host, reborn in their descendants, would have to fight once more. And this time…

The battle would decide the fate of Earth itself.

Dr. Astrid Jorgensen had always believed in reason. Her life had been defined by facts, by records, by digging into the remnants of history to uncover the truth. Myths and legends had fascinated her, but she had always approached them with skepticism, viewing ancient tales as exaggerated fragments of forgotten events. That belief had sustained her for years, until now. Because when she awoke on the sixth night after the Zepharians' return, the world felt… different.

At first, it was subtle, just a faint sense that something was off. The air smelled sharper, as though the frost carried the scent of iron and earth. The morning light spilling through her window seemed too vivid, colors too bright, too rich. The shadows along her walls seemed to move strangely, flickering like flames even though the morning sun had risen.

And the sounds...
She could hear the subtle crackle of embers in her fireplace, though the flames had died hours ago. She heard the drip of melting ice sliding off her roof, the rustling of leaves outside her sealed window. Even her own heartbeat seemed louder, pounding steadily inside her chest like the echo of a distant war drum.

Confused, Astrid sat on the edge of her bed, pressing a hand to her temple.

"You're tired," she told herself. "Exhaustion... nothing more."

But the moment she lowered her hand, she saw them.

The faintest glow danced along her skin, barely visible at first. She blinked, certain her eyes were playing tricks on her. But no... There they were, runes, faintly etched into the flesh of her forearms. The symbols seemed to pulse beneath her skin, glowing with an eerie silver-blue light.

She knew these symbols. They were from the Elder Futhark, the runic alphabet of her Viking ancestors. Astrid staggered back, her breath catching in her throat.

"No... It's not possible."

She stumbled into her bathroom, wrenching back the sleeve of her sweater and thrusting her arm beneath the harsh glare of the mirror's light. The runes seemed to shift, as though they were... alive. The lines pulsed like veins, faint patterns rippling just beneath the surface of her skin.

"What is happening to me?" she whispered.

And then, a voice spoke inside her mind.

"Astrid..."

The voice was deep, powerful, like thunder rolling through distant mountains.

"Daughter of the lost... the time has come."

Her vision blurred. The world twisted, colors bending and warping like smoke caught in the wind. And for a fleeting moment, she was no longer in her home.

In an instant, she stood upon a battlefield, not of Earth, but of some far-distant place, a world torn by war. The air was thick with ash and fire, the sky above splintered by streaks of crimson light. Ships the size of mountains loomed in the distance, their hulls marked with the same glowing runes that now burned upon her arms. Warriors clashed in the distance, men clad in Viking armor, their shields reinforced with alien metals, their swords humming with energy.

They fought against something... monstrous. The enemy surged in masses, dark, writhing creatures, their bodies twisted and amorphous, shifting shapes as they moved. The air itself seemed to die around them, as if the very presence of these creatures drained the light from existence.

A black mass pulsed at the heart of chaos, the Svarthjarta, the Black Heart, devouring everything in its path. It did not kill. It unmade. Ships dissolved to dust mid-flight. Light turned black and collapsed into silence. No cries. No pain.

Just... nothing. It moved like a thought never spoken aloud, a whisper of the end written into the bones of the universe.

And in the center of it all, a figure stood atop a massive, broken warship. He was tall, armored in blackened steel, with a thick auburn beard streaked silver with age. In his hand, he held a great axe, glowing faintly with blue runes that seemed to repel the darkness. Astrid knew him. Even through the haze of battle, his face was unmistakable, Erik Bloodaxe.

The warlord king turned, his piercing blue eyes glowing like twin flames. And those eyes locked directly onto hers.

Erik's gaze bored into her with such intensity that her chest tightened, her breath coming in ragged gasps.

"You are not ready yet."

His voice echoed in her mind, distant yet undeniable.
And then, the vision shattered.

Astrid staggered back into her study, her legs buckling beneath her. Her desk struck her hip, and her scattered papers went flying across the floor. Her breathing was rapid, her heartbeat thundering in her ears. The warmth of the runes still pulsed beneath her skin, like embers waiting to ignite. She stared down at her trembling hands.

She had spent her life undoing myths. Now she was becoming one. The runes weren't symbols. They were sentences written on her skin by a story that started before she was born.

"What... what is happening to me?"

Her mind refused to answer. All she could feel was the lingering presence of Erik Bloodaxe's gaze, still burning in her mind's eye. He had looked at her not with anger, nor with pity, but with something far worse, expectation. And somehow, deep within her soul, Astrid knew that whatever was coming… She was destined to face it.

Astrid was not alone. All over the world, others were awakening. At first, the changes seemed isolated, whispered rumors of individuals claiming to hear phantom voices, reporting visions of forgotten battles, or noticing strange symbols appearing on their skin.

But soon, it became clear that this was no isolated phenomenon; it was a global awakening. Men and women, all of Norse descent, were experiencing the same unexplained phenomenon.

In the remote villages of Norway, elderly fishermen stumbled home from icy waters, their backs once bent by time now straightened, their old joints somehow restored. Some claimed they could see storms before they arrived, others claimed they could predict the movements of fish and animals, as though nature itself whispered to them.

In the frigid peaks of Iceland, sheep herders awoke to find runes glowing along their forearms, and when they followed those symbols to their meanings, they uncovered forgotten Viking relics hidden in the soil — tools, weapons, and carved stones that seemed to hum with unknown energy.

Meanwhile, in the heart of New York City, a young man working construction single-handedly lifted a steel beam meant for five men. His coworkers swore they had seen runes flicker along his neck just before he grabbed the beam. In Berlin, a woman working as a linguist discovered that she could suddenly read runic inscriptions without hesitation, inscriptions historians had struggled to decipher for decades. And in the Arctic territories of Russia, a retired soldier claimed he had been hunted by shadows, creatures of smoke and shifting darkness that only retreated when the symbols on his arm blazed with light. All of them, men and women alike, shared one undeniable truth: They were changing.

Their bodies had grown stronger. Their memories had begun to fill with foreign thoughts and instincts, memories that seemed to come not from their own lives, but from distant ancestors. They were no longer fully human. But perhaps... they never had been.

It became clear that something buried deep within their DNA, something ancient, something forgotten, had been activated. The genetic sequence had lain dormant for generations, passed down quietly through the bloodlines of those whose ancestors had once sailed with Erik Bloodaxe.

This dormant code was no simple mutation. It was something... designed. It had waited. Watched. And now, at a time when the world stood at the brink of war with the Svarthjarta, the Black Heart, the Descendants were being called back to their purpose.

The legacy of Erik Bloodaxe's warriors had been woven into their blood, waiting for the right moment to stir. And that moment had come.

It didn't take long before the world's intelligence agencies noticed. At first, the reports were fragmented, unexplained genetic mutations, ordinary people suddenly displaying inhuman strength, heightened senses, or visions of alien battlefields. But when these cases continued to grow, appearing in dozens of nations, governments realized it was too widespread to ignore.

The world divided. Some governments saw the Awakened as a threat, the early stages of an invasion, or perhaps the makings of a new species that could outpace humanity itself. Others viewed them as an opportunity, a force that could be harnessed, trained, and weaponized for global dominance. Fearing what they could not understand, governments around the world began rounding up the Awakened.

Secret facilities were established to study these "Descendants". In some cases, individuals went willingly, believing they were helping to uncover the truth of their ancestry. Scientists examined their blood, their brains, and their mysterious new abilities. But in other cases... They were not given a choice.

Men in unmarked vehicles snatched Descendants from their homes. Families reported missing loved ones, no notes, no messages. Entire villages in northern Scandinavia were quietly erased, the government offering vague statements about "military operations" to explain their absence.

The world's leaders feared what these descendants might become. Would they grow into something unstoppable, a race of warriors too powerful to control? Would they rise against humanity, a species that had long forgotten its place in the stars?

Fear spread through the public. Protesters marched through the streets, demanding answers.

Religious leaders claimed the Descendants were agents of Ragnarok, sent to destroy humanity. Others believed they were gifts from the gods, destined to defend the world from the approaching threat.

Through it all, the Zepharians stood silently. They made no attempt to explain the awakening. They gave no warning of what was to come. They merely watched, like guardians awaiting a storm they had long known would arrive. And far beyond the Earth's atmosphere, the Zepharian fleet continued to hold formation, their ships hovering silently, glowing runes etched into their hulls like distant stars.

Whatever they knew, whatever they were waiting for, it was clear they believed that Earth's only hope lay not with its armies, nor with its weapons... But with the descendants of Erik Bloodaxe's lost warriors. And soon, the Awakened would have to answer that call.

The world's Awakened stood at a crossroads. For some, the changes they had experienced, the strength, the sharpened senses, the flickering memories of lives never lived, felt like a gift. A blessing from their Viking ancestors, a power to be wielded with pride.

These individuals saw themselves as the heirs to something greater than themselves, guardians of an ancient bloodline, champions of a forgotten purpose.

In the frozen towns of Norway, men and women gathered in ancient halls, lifting drinking horns in reverence to the old gods. They carved fresh runes into wooden beams, burning the marks of Thor, Tyr, and Odin into their walls. They trained in the ways of their forebears, wielding axes and blades, certain that whatever storm was coming, they were destined to stand and fight.

But for others, the awakening brought fear. These individuals whispered to priests and doctors, desperate to be cured. They had seen visions of flaming battlefields, of alien ships blotting out the sky. They believed that the power awakening within them was unnatural, something that should never have been stirred. And then, there were those who turned their fear into violence.

Armed groups emerged in cities across the world, convinced that the Awakened were an infection, a threat to humanity itself. These extremists hunted those they believed carried

the curse of the Vikings, believing them to be the harbingers
of a war that could doom the Earth.

The world was fracturing. And still... the Svarthjarta waited.
It had felt their awakening. It knew they were no longer
hidden. And now... it was hungry.

The storm that had been brewing in silence finally broke on
the tenth night after the Zepharians' warning. It began not
with an attack, nor with a whisper, but with a war cry. Not
on Earth. But from the stars themselves.

It appeared in the sky over Norway, spiraling out of the cold
void of space like a storm rolling in over the mountains. The
air shuddered as the sky split open, a jagged seam of light
that spilled across the heavens. Out of that gaping wound,
ships emerged, massive warships, their hulls gleaming with
both Norse runes and alien technology.

The Viking warships descended. No engines. No rockets. No
atmospheric burn. They simply... appeared, riding channels
of folded space as if they had been there all along, waiting in
the seams of reality.

The ships were like none Earth's militaries had ever seen,
curved vessels of impossible metal, glowing veins of blue
light weaving through their surface like molten steel. At their
prows, massive dragon-headed carvings opened their jaws,
spitting flickers of golden flame as they sailed through the
sky.

The runes etched into their hulls glowed brighter than fire,
radiating power that felt ancient and endless. This was no
ordinary fleet.

At the heart of the fleet sailed a great black warship, larger
than all the rest. Its hull was carved with the symbol of
Yggdrasil, the World Tree, encircled by a great serpent

devouring its own tail. The lead ship was called Naglfari, named for the vessel of nightmares in Norse myth, was a seamless blend of ancient and otherworldly, carved with the faces of dragons and wolves, shimmering like moonstone.

On its deck stood a figure cloaked in shadow, clad in armor forged from both Viking steel and alien alloys. His face was obscured by a helmet marked with the symbol of Odin's eye, and a massive war axe hung at his side. He stepped forward, standing beneath the flickering runes that blazed above him.

The world watched as his image was broadcast across every screen, every device. No camera captured the transmission; it simply appeared, burning through airwaves, data streams, and satellites.

His voice was deep, commanding, yet strangely intimate. And when he spoke, his voice thundered through every mind on Earth, as though the words had been carved into the marrow of their bones:

"The time for sleep has ended, descendants of Midgard, of the Axe, of the Lost. You were never meant to die as humans. You were meant to rise as gods. Descendants of the Bloodaxe... it is time to remember who you are."

His words shook the air, vibrating through cities and villages alike. Across the world, those who had awakened felt their runic marks ignite, burning like embers beneath their skin. Some fell to their knees, clutching their arms in awe and fear. Others stood tall, feeling a surge of purpose, as though the blood of their ancestors was calling them home.

The Zepharians had stood by in silence since their return. But now, as the Viking fleet split the heavens, they moved. Their ships rose from Earth's atmosphere, gliding into defensive formations like the rows of a shield wall. But they did not attack. They waited.

And those who had experienced visions and those who had seen the flickering glimpses of the coming war knew what was coming next. This fleet had not come as invaders. They had come as warriors, the lost kin of Erik Bloodaxe, returning to Earth because they knew one thing for certain. The Svarthjarta, the Black Heart, was coming. And this war was only just beginning.

Chapter 7: Unraveling the Past

The sky burned. Not with fire, but with runed light but a celestial tapestry of sigils and aurora, stretching across the heavens as if the gods themselves had returned. A shimmering host of long-lost ships descended like stars reborn, their hulls humming with power both ancient and unknown.

The Lost Viking Fleet, whispered of in poems and fevered dreams, had come back from the void. The ships, Drakenskip reborn, no longer sailed water, but the currents of space. Forged not from wood and iron, but from alloys that shimmered like obsidian and silver under moonlight. The hulls pulsed with rivers of blue light—Norse runes braided with Zepharian glyphs, like the old gods had married the stars.

The air on Earth felt denser, heavier, as if the atmosphere itself recognized the power that hovered above. At the lead of the formation, a single great warship loomed larger than the rest, its silhouette shaped like a dragon poised to strike. From its forward deck, a figure emerged: massive, wrapped in armor that fused fur-lined leather with flowing alien metal. His horned helm bore the mark of Odin's Eye, a single glowing rune etched into the brow.

And then, he raised an armored hand. Across the Earth, descendants froze. Something inside them shifted, a weight uncoiling from bloodlines that had waited a thousand years to awaken. It wasn't magic. It wasn't technology. It was a memory. A call to arms, not heard through ears but felt through bones.

"You are not just of Earth. You are born of the old gods and the long stars. Remember who you are."

The voice rang through the minds of the Awakened, not a command, but a truth.

Dr. Astrid Jorgensen dropped the ancient ring she'd been cataloging. It hit the tile with a sharp clink, spinning wildly before settling near her feet. But she barely noticed.

Her chest clenched as a presence filled her. Her vision blurred, not with dizziness, but with remembrance. Suddenly, she was no longer in her Oslo study. The books vanished. The walls dissolved. She stood on an alien plain, beneath a purple sky cracked by fire and starships.

In the distance, twin moons hung like broken shields, and below them… war. Vikings, no, warriors in Norse armor enhanced with alien craftsmanship, clashed with shadows that bled smoke and screamed with inhuman shrieks. The air reeked of ozone and iron.

She looked down. Her hands gripped a battle-axe, not forged in any Earthly forge. Blue light pulsed along its blade. Armor covered her body, shaped to her form, carved with runes she didn't recall learning, but understood.
Astrid—no, someone else—charged.

Beside her, other warriors moved in formation, a shield wall of light and fury, smashing into the advancing dark. She could feel the rhythm of war—the timing, the unity. The life she had known was gone. This was real. This was home. And in the center of it all, Erik Bloodaxe.

Towering. Immortal. The axe in his hands hissed with burning ice. His eyes locked onto hers—not in confusion, but recognition.

"We ride again, daughter of Jorgens. But not yet."

And just like that, she was back. Collapsed against her desk, her breath ragged. Her arms glowing faintly beneath her sleeves, the runes pulsing in time with her heart. The ring lay motionless at her feet. She knew. She wasn't hallucinating. She wasn't dreaming. She was remembering.

Astrid wasn't the only one. She read the reports. Thousands now. Across every continent. The map looked like a constellation drawn from Norse bloodlines. It was happening faster than anyone could control.

Across Earth, others were pulled into the current of something vast and ancient, as if a cosmic tide had begun to surge beneath the skin of the world.

In a windswept outpost in northern Iceland, a woman named Yrsa Bjornsdottir dropped the net she had cast into a frozen inlet. The sea steamed beneath her feet, though the temperature was sub-zero. Her breath hung in the air, glowing faintly. The others in her village stared, but Yrsa simply closed her eyes and whispered, "He's here."

On the steppes of Mongolia, a young man of Norwegian descent—Leif Stiansen, adopted as a child—collapsed during a wrestling match. When he woke, his skin bore spiraling runes across his spine, and his eyes had turned a ghostly shade of blue. He spoke perfect Old Norse, a language no one had taught him.

In Osaka, a physics professor descended from Scandinavian traders screamed as she was pulled from a dream of sailing through asteroid fields in a ship carved like a wolf's head. When she woke, she scrawled equations of star-folding and zero-point energy she had no way of knowing.

Each descendant was changed in different ways. Some gained strength. Others knowledge. Some heard voices. Some saw futures. But all of them felt the same thing: A call. From something beyond Earth. And from something drawing near.

The Zepharians observed without interference. Their vessels, once enigmatic curiosities, had now positioned themselves in synchronized orbit around the planet. To the naked eye, they looked like runic constellations, points of light that pulsed in geometric rhythm. No messages came from them. No actions. They simply watched. And humanity… grew restless.

Governments around the world divided along lines of fear and ambition. The United Nations convened an emergency council. Satellites were redirected. Fighter jets were scrambled. And still, the Zepharians did nothing.

At a NATO briefing in Brussels, a general slammed his fist on the table. "If these people are being activated—if they're developing new abilities—we need containment. Quarantine. Preemptive security measures."

Across the table, a scientist, Dr. Helena Akesson, herself an Awakened, spoke through clenched teeth. "They are not weapons. They are people. You don't even understand what you're dealing with."

"Exactly," the general snapped. "That's the problem."

And no one knew what would happen when the Svarthjarta arrived. Astrid did know one thing, the answer was with Eric Bloodaxe in Hafrsfjord.

Eight hours later, Astrid stood on the shores of Hafrsfjord, where the first kings of Norway had once unified the land in fire and steel. Now, history threatened to repeat itself, not with men, but with legends.

The air was thick with anticipation. Around her stood dozens of Awakened, some young, some old, all wearing expressions that danced between awe and dread. A humming sound, low and primal, rose from the fjord as the massive warship descended. Its reflection shimmered on the glass-like water, casting runes across the snow-dusted rocks. A ramp descended, not with a hiss of hydraulics, but a deep thrum, like a battle drum from the bones of the world. He appeared through the mist. Erik Bloodaxe.

The warlord walked with the weight of centuries in his stride. His armor was dark, carved in overlapping plates of alien alloy. The great axe strapped to his back pulsed with light, and his eyes, blue like the Arctic sky, locked directly on Astrid. He looked at her not as a ghost, but as a torch-passer. She was not meant to worship him, she was meant to finish what he began.

"Jorgensen's blood... You carry it well."

Astrid opened her mouth, but no words came. She had imagined this moment a thousand ways, in dreams, in study, in fear. None of them captured the gravity of reality.

"Why me?" she asked finally.

Erik stepped closer, his breath frosting the air.

"Because the echoes chose you. Because you remember. Because the blood of kings runs louder in your veins than most."

He lifted a hand. Astrid flinched, then realized he wasn't reaching for her. He was summoning something. A glimmer formed between them, runic light swirling, solidifying. A memory made manifest. A vision of a training hall carved into a mountainside, filled with warriors sparring, chanting, transforming.

"You will rebuild this," he said. "You will awaken the rest."

Within days, the Skjaldskapa, the first of the new warrior halls, was established in the Norwegian highlands, hidden beneath a mountain once believed dormant. Inside, Zepharian and Norse architecture melded: wooden beams etched with sagas joined alien alloys that defied gravity. The Awakened came in waves.

They trained in disciplines they didn't know they remembered, bladed combat, energy manipulation, mental focus rituals passed down from warrior-priests who had fought in distant starfields. Astrid walked among them, now no longer an observer. She learned to wield an axe with a blade of pure light. She felt her body grow stronger, not from exercise, but from alignment. Her mind sharpened. She no longer dreamed of Erik. She dreamed with him.

Not all welcomed this rebirth. In Washington, Beijing, and Moscow, distrust turned to fear. Surveillance operations escalated. Secret orders were passed down.

"We cannot allow another race to surpass us," a Chinese general said during a closed-door meeting. "Even if they are our own."

In the United States, the formation of Project Heimdall signaled the first formal attempt to control or eliminate unregistered Awakened. Raids began. Camps were established. Some Awakened went into hiding. Others... fought back.

A violent clash broke out in Berlin, where Awakened protestors resisted arrest by a private defense contractor. Three died. Runes carved into the cobblestone streets with blood still glowed the next morning.

The Zepharians issued a single, silent warning. A ship hovered over each capital city for one hour. No threats. No communication. Just presence. And then... they vanished again.

On the outer rim of the solar system, where ancient probes drifted like ghosts, the first anomaly appeared. A tear in space. Small. Silent. But growing. The Svarthjarta had arrived.

Astrid felt it before the news reached her. A cold pressure in her chest. The dreams shifted. The skies above burned darker. That night, she stood beside Erik, both staring into the fire at the center of Skjaldskapa.

He spoke without looking at her. "When it comes, it will not arrive with thunder. It will arrive like rot. Silent. Corrupting. Feeding."

Astrid nodded. "Then we'll carve it out."

Erik turned, and for the first time, he smiled.

"A true daughter of the Axe."

The call went out, and the Awakened came. From every continent, those marked by the runes made pilgrimage to the ancient valley of Ydalir, long believed myth. Nestled between peaks in the highlands of Norway, the valley had been cloaked for centuries—shielded by Zepharian technology, hidden in plain sight. Now, it pulsed with life.

Over a thousand gathered in the newly erected amphitheater of stone and steel, beneath a sky alive with runes that danced in violet and gold. The air thrummed with expectation. This was not a coronation. It was a council of awakening.

Erik Bloodaxe stood at the center on a raised stone dais, flanked by his lieutenants:

Gunnar Flame-Eye, the berserker who had survived the fall of Rigel-9.

Yrsa Shieldbreaker, reborn after the Siege of Mimir's Gate And now, Astrid Jorgensen, newly chosen Keeper of Memory.

They addressed the gathered: warriors, scholars, children, and newly awakened civilians whose lives had turned inside out.

"We stand on the edge of a storm," Erik declared. "The world you knew is ending. But the world we carry in our blood... is rising."

But unity would not come easily. From among the Awakened, dissent grew. A young leader named Soren Blackhand, a former marine from Canada, stood and raised a clenched fist. His arm shimmered with blackened runes— ones not found in any historical record.

"You speak of destiny," he said, voice loud. "But some of us weren't warriors. Some of us were farmers. Teachers. Why should we fight a war we didn't choose?"

Murmurs rippled through the amphitheater. Others nodded. Erik did not answer. Astrid stepped forward instead.

"You were born from bloodlines that crossed the stars. You carry the weapons of ancestors who held back the dark. You may not want this war. But it wants you."

Silence fell. And then, softly, Soren spoke again.

"Then teach us. Or let us die with purpose."

That night, beneath the shifting light of the auroras, a sudden boom echoed across the mountains. An explosion rocked a nearby ridge. Dozens raced to investigate. What they found chilled them. A drone, Earth-made, had struck a shielding tower, one that cloaked the Skjaldskapa's defenses. A message had been embedded in the wreckage.

"We see you. Stand down or be removed."
—Project Heimdall

The war had begun, not with the Svarthjarta, but with fearful people.

In response, the Zepharians activated Earth's first World-Ward, a barrier not seen since the fall of Alfheim's orbitals. It shimmered like liquid glass above the clouds, unseen by satellites, pulsing in harmony with the Earth's magnetic field. It would protect the Awakened—for now. But Astrid knew the shield could not last forever.

She stood on the high ledge at Ydalir, watching the shield flare above. Behind her, young Awakened trained by torchlight. She could hear them sparring, laughing, struggling. Becoming. Beside her, Erik stepped close.

"This is only the beginning," he said.

She nodded, her voice quiet but resolute.

"Then we fight for what comes after."

And far beyond Earth, in the black folds of space, the Svarthjarta opened another eye. It had found them.

The blood had remembered. The runes had returned. And across the world, the descendants of Midgard stirred, not as relics of the past, but as warriors of what was to come.

Chapter 8: Clash of Cultures

The return of the Lost Vikings had shattered the world's perception of history, of identity, and of the place of humanity in the grand cosmic order.

The revelation that an entire civilization of Norse warriors had not perished, but had instead left Earth to prepare for an ancient war, one that now threatened to return, sent shockwaves through governments, religious institutions, and the scientific community.

The U.S. called it a bio-psychic anomaly. Russia began drafting laws labeling 'genetic awakenings' as military assets. Iceland declared the descendants national treasures. And Norway? Norway was afraid. Because deep down... they believed.

They called them anachronisms. Relics in fur and iron. But they weren't. They were continuity. Blood that never stopped remembering. And when a UN general mocked a descendant's braided hair, that descendant shattered his desk in half with a single strike, and never broke eye contact.

The world was no longer just the world. It was part of something much greater. And not everyone was ready to accept that truth.

The convoy of black SUVs wound its way through the icy roads leading into Ydalir Valley, tires crunching against frost and gravel. Frostbitten pine trees lined the route like silent sentinels. Inside the lead vehicle, a translator fidgeted with her headset as the Norwegian Prime Minister, Maren Klev, sat in quiet contemplation. Her breath fogged the tinted window as she stared at the distant silhouettes of structures, angular, gleaming, and entirely alien, rising from the ancient valley.

"They call it a sanctuary," said the translator, reading a briefing. "But we have no idea how long it's been here. Sensors couldn't even detect it until last week."

Klev didn't answer right away. She adjusted the sleeves of her coat, concealing the faint glow of a rune that had started appearing on her left wrist the night before.

"I don't think we found it," she said finally. "I think it allowed itself to be seen."

As they crossed the final ridge, the valley opened below, sprawling, otherworldly. Viking banners snapped in the wind next to Zepharian pylons that shimmered like glass threads. Training circles, weapons forges, meditation chambers—it looked like something out of a fever dream. A medieval fortress crash-landed into a science fiction prophecy.

And in the center of it all, Erik Bloodaxe stood on a raised platform, eyes fixed on the incoming convoy. He turned to Astrid Jorgensen beside him and said with a trace of amusement, "And so the high kings of this new world arrive... in wagons of steel."

Astrid smirked, but the expression didn't reach her eyes. She could feel the tension building like thunderclouds behind her ribs. These weren't just visitors—they were heads of state, military commanders, and scientists carrying the full weight of a world terrified of what they didn't understand. And now, they had come face to face with legends reborn.

"You might want to choose your words carefully," she muttered. "They're not here for poetry."

"They are not here for truth either," Erik said. "They come to measure us. To decide whether to kneel... or to strike."

The convoy came to a halt, and doors opened with soft mechanical hisses. Armed guards in high-tech armor stepped out first, followed by world leaders, Klev from Norway, a French diplomat, two American generals, and a Chinese envoy with unreadable eyes. Each wore the same mixture of disbelief and caution.

The air was colder here, not just in temperature but in tone. The valley felt like it existed outside of time, like Earth itself wasn't sure it should be touching this place.

Astrid stepped forward to meet them, her posture straight, diplomatic, but laced with quiet power. She wore her research jacket over reinforced leather, a symbol of both worlds. Her eyes swept across the delegation.

"Welcome to Ydalir," she said. "You're standing on ground that hasn't been seen by modern man for over a thousand years."

"And yet it looks like a staging ground," one of the generals said, eyeing the distant Zepharian towers warily.

"It's a training ground," Astrid corrected. "And training is what keeps war at bay."

No one spoke immediately. Then Erik stepped beside her, towering over everyone, his armor humming with faint energy. His voice rolled like thunder.

"Speak your minds. We have little time for subtlety."

The delegation hesitated. No one had expected Erik Bloodaxe to look so... alive. So human, yet so obviously something more. His presence had gravity. Not political, but visceral, like standing too close to a wildfire and pretending you weren't afraid.

Prime Minister Klev stepped forward first, flanked by two aides and a security officer scanning the surroundings with a portable sensor. She nodded once toward Astrid, then turned to Erik.

"You are not what we expected," she said in Norwegian. Her voice carried weight, but not arrogance. "We came prepared to deal with an incursion, not a resurrection."

Erik let out a dry laugh. "And yet here I stand. Not as ghost, but as storm."

Beside him, Astrid translated quickly for the others. The French diplomat narrowed his eyes, scribbling notes into a sleek tablet. One of the American generals, General Wallace, Astrid recalled, folded his arms.

"We need answers," Wallace said. "What are you building here? What is this fleet planning? Who are these 'Awakened' you're recruiting from our nations?"

Astrid didn't flinch. "You're asking the wrong questions. What you should be asking is: What are we preparing for?"

Wallace's expression tightened. "Are you saying there's a threat?"

"No," Erik replied, stepping forward, his eyes piercing. "I am saying the threat is already coming. Your governments just haven't been able to see it yet."

The Chinese envoy, silent until now, raised a brow. "And we're to believe this? Based on prophecy? On dreams?"

Astrid gestured toward the towering Zepharian pylons. "No. Based on readings from your own orbital telescopes. Ask your astrophysicists about the distortion approaching from outside Saturn's orbit. We didn't cause that. But we've seen it before."

She tried to explain to both sides. That the war wasn't a myth, that the warriors weren't delusional. But neither side wanted nuance. One saw madness. The other saw weakness.

The delegation fell quiet. Because they had seen it too. They just hadn't known what it meant, until now.

The wind shifted, carrying the distant sound of steel clashing against steel. Awakened warriors sparring near the training circles. It reminded Astrid of old poems where gods trained in hidden realms before Ragnarök. Except now, they weren't stories. They were schedules. Rotations. Tactical briefings. Real.

Prime Minister Klev broke the silence. "You claim to be preparing for a war that none of our intelligence agencies can verify. A war against something no nation recognizes."

Erik's eyes narrowed. "Your nations do not recognize it because they no longer listen to their dead. But we do. And they are screaming."

Astrid stepped forward, softer. "It's not a question of belief. It's a question of time. We're tracking the Svarthjarta. We have data. Patterns. The Zepharians have confirmed its advance through multiple systems—worlds that no longer exist. We're not asking for your armies. We're asking you to stay out of our way long enough to stop this."

Wallace scoffed. "You're asking the world to step aside while you gather genetically enhanced warriors, forge unknown weapons, and orbit ancient warships over sovereign nations."

Erik's voice cut through like a blade. "We do not ask. We offer. What you do with that offering determines whether your species dies in ignorance... or survives with purpose."

The Chinese envoy tilted his head. "And what if we say no?"

Astrid glanced at Erik, but he said nothing. She answered instead.

"Then you'll be the first to fall."

The words settled like dust on steel. No threat, just inevitability. The truth was: they didn't need Earth's approval. They needed time. And that was running out.

The delegation was escorted deeper into the valley. As they walked, the clash of ideology grew louder than the footsteps on stone. Leaders murmured to aides, diplomats exchanged anxious glances, and the military personnel kept their hands near holstered weapons. But what truly disturbed them were the sights.

A dozen Awakened children, no older than ten, ran through a courtyard chasing a hovering, rune-inscribed disc that blinked in response to their laughter. A young boy leapt higher than gravity should allow, caught the disc mid-air, and landed in a crouch like a trained gymnast.

Johan was a codebreaker from Bergen. He'd never held an axe in his life. But now the runes burned beneath his skin, and he couldn't stop dreaming of screaming across alien fields with blood on his hands. He hated it. Hated what it meant. But every night the dreams came clearer. And his hands... they started to itch for steel."

In another corner, a woman in Zepharian robes taught a group of adult Awakened to channel energy through their limbs, guiding it through neural pathways awakened by rune etching.

General Wallace broke the silence. "You're building an army."

Astrid didn't look at him. "We're building a civilization."

They passed an enormous mural carved into the cliff face. It depicted Norse warriors in battle against swirling void-creatures, joined by luminous Zepharian figures. The mural spanned nearly fifty meters, and its last panel showed Earth, a small blue marble, encased in a glowing sphere of runes. A warning. Or a promise. Prime Minister Klev stopped to study it.

"How much of this is prophecy?" she asked. "And how much is memory?"

"Both," Erik said. "There are truths so old they become stories. And stories so strong they become weapons."

Suddenly, one of the American intelligence officers muttered into his comm. His eyes widened. He turned to Wallace.

"Sir, NORAD just detected an anomaly entering the outer solar system. Gravitational field irregularities. Pulses matching deep-void signatures."

Astrid's blood ran cold.

"How far?" she asked.

"Somewhere near Neptune. Maybe closer."

Everyone looked up. The sky was still calm. But the darkness was coming.

Later that evening, the delegation gathered in a domed chamber carved into the side of the mountain—a fusion of Viking hall and alien observatory. A central firepit burned with blue flame, casting shifting shadows across the stone walls. Above, the dome projected a holographic view of the solar system. At the edge of the projection: a blot of writhing black, slowly bleeding toward Earth.

"This is a live feed," Astrid explained. "We've synchronized our sensors with the Zepharian observation lattice surrounding the solar system. That mass is… growing."

The French diplomat leaned forward. "It looks… alive."

"It is," said a voice from the shadows.

A woman stepped into the firelight, Yrsa Shieldbreaker, her armor scorched from battle drills, her hair bound in silver cords. She carried a two-headed axe on her back and a gaze that made generals look away.

"It does not come with reason. It comes with hunger. The Svarthjarta consumes not just worlds, but memory. Culture. Light. It leaves behind silence."

Prime Minister Klev looked toward Astrid. "Why haven't you brought this to the UN?"

"We did," Astrid said flatly. "Three years ago. They called it cosmic radiation noise. They buried it in a think tank in Geneva."

There was a pause, then General Wallace spoke again, quieter this time. "So what now? You've made your sanctuary, trained your people. But what if we're too late?" Erik stepped forward. "Then we die with axes in our hands, as our fathers did."

Yrsa added, "But we don't plan to die. We plan to win."

A new projection rippled through the dome, one of an Earth wreathed in protective runes, a fleet surrounding it in formation, and fire raining down from the heavens. A vision. A warning. A plan. The room fell silent again. But no one doubted anymore that war was coming.

That night, Astrid wandered alone through the valley. Training had stopped. The Zepharian lights dimmed in reverence. Even the night birds seemed subdued. The sky above, brilliant with stars, now felt… thinner. As if the universe had drawn in its breath.

She passed the quiet forge where sparks usually danced. A solitary figure stood near the embers—Eirik Vostov, a recently Awakened engineer-turned-warrior, sharpening a blade that hummed faintly with runic energy.

"They're afraid," he said without looking at her.

Astrid stopped beside him. "The delegates?"

"All of them. Even us. Especially us."

She nodded, folding her arms. "It's different when you know what's coming. It stops being a story and becomes a timeline."

Eirik turned, his eyes glowing softly beneath a fur-lined hood. "Do you believe we can win?"

Astrid hesitated. "I believe we must. And that's enough for now."

He offered a wry smile. "Spoken like a Bloodaxe."

She arched an eyebrow. "I'm a Jorgensen."

Eirik slid the blade back into its sheath. "You carry both."

Above them, a Zepharian ship passed silently overhead, casting a ripple of light across the stones. It made no sound, but its shadow whispered of speed, of purpose. Somewhere aboard, Zepharian strategists were already mapping possible outcomes, counting variables in probabilities beyond human comprehension.

Astrid looked up and whispered, "Then let them count on us."

At dawn, the delegation prepared to depart. The world outside still held its breath, unaware of the truths exchanged in the depths of the valley. Diplomatic language would later sanitize the encounter—phrases like "preliminary cooperation," "shared concerns," and "further investigation."

But those who had stood before Erik Bloodaxe, before the projections of cosmic annihilation, would never be the same. Before they left, Astrid requested a private audience with Prime Minister Klev. They stood near the edge of the high cliffs overlooking Ydalir, mist curling up from the valley below.

"You're one of us," Astrid said quietly. "I saw the rune on your wrist."

Klev didn't deny it. She pulled back her sleeve, revealing a glowing mark shaped like a spiral sun. "It started as a bruise. Then it... changed."

"You'll dream soon," Astrid said. "You'll see where we're headed."

Klev's breath misted in the cold air. "And if I don't like what I see?"

Astrid looked out across the awakening world below. "Then you'll have a choice. But it won't change what's coming."

Klev sighed. "I still represent a sovereign government."

"I know," Astrid said. "But what's coming won't recognize flags. Or borders. Or fear."

Klev studied her for a long time. Then nodded.

"I'll keep your secret... for now. But the world won't wait forever."

Astrid watched her leave. Erik stepped up beside her, silent.

"She'll come around," he said.

"She already has," Astrid replied. "She just doesn't know it yet."

They stood side by side, watching the world prepare for war and for rebirth. Above them, in the far reaches of the void, the stars began to blink... one by one.

A week later, the first rift opened. It wasn't large, barely the size of a passenger jet, but it was visible from orbit, and unmistakably unnatural. A gash of darkness carved into space, not simply void but anti-light, flickering like the edge of an unlit fire.

Every sensor on Earth reacted instantly. Satellites failed. Communications glitched. Migratory birds changed course. Tides warped. And in the heart of the Arctic Circle, inside an underground Zepharian relay station, alarms screamed in tones no human throat could reproduce.

Astrid watched the projections from a reinforced observation room beneath Ydalir. Holograms displayed the growing distortion near Pluto's orbit, and early data coming from lunar telescopes showed gravitational lensing inconsistent with any known mass.

"It's not just a portal," said Ragnald Steinsson, a physicist-turned-Watcher whose rune had appeared across the back of his neck like a branching tree. "It's a mouth. And it's opening."

Yrsa joined them at the console, her expression grim. "Then it's not long now."

"How long until it reaches Earth?" Astrid asked.

Ragnald shook his head. "It won't have to. Not if we don't stop what comes through."

Across the globe, governments began to mobilize, but no one could agree on what to prepare for. Some stockpiled weapons. Others activated planetary defense grids. A few still refused to acknowledge the threat at all.

The world had always been divided by beliefs. But the Svarthjarta would not care what humanity believed. It would only consume.

That night, the skies over Ydalir danced with a furious aurora, bright greens laced with streaks of crimson and violet, as though the heavens themselves had begun to bleed. Warriors stood at the cliff's edge in silence, staring upward. Some clutched weapons. Others whispered prayers. A few simply waited, their bodies taut with anticipation. In the great hall beneath the mountain, Erik Bloodaxe met with his inner circle.

The table before them glowed with Zepharian glyphs, each node representing a possible timeline. None were without fire.

"We need more time," said Astrid. "We're training hundreds, but if this escalates, we'll need thousands."

"We may not get thousands," Yrsa replied. "But we will get the right ones."

Erik stood, placing both hands on the table. "The rift is only the beginning. Before the first shadow lands, we must be ready to bring the storm to it."

Astrid looked at the models—Earth surrounded by flickering sigils, fleets poised like sharpened teeth.
"What about the rest of humanity?" she asked quietly.

"They're still divided."

"They always will be," Erik said. "Until the fire forges them."

And in the deepest reaches of the void, something turned its gaze toward them. A hunger older than galaxies. A presence darker than death. And it whispered a single truth into the dreams of those who dared to resist:

"You were not meant to rise.
You were meant to be forgotten."

But they would not be forgotten. They would be remembered, in fire, in steel, in blood, and in light.
Because the clash of cultures was over. Now came the clash of worlds.

Chapter 9: The Diverse Earth

The world was no longer united. The awakening of the Descendants, the return of the Warborn, and the undeniable presence of Zepharian vessels over Earth's skies had fractured humanity along deep cultural, political, and philosophical fault lines.

In Oslo, a once-celebrated peace summit devolved into shouting matches as diplomats hurled accusations across the room. In Shanghai, holographic billboards alternated between warnings of alien invasion and depictions of Warborn warriors protecting children from projected beasts of shadow. In Washington, protests surged outside the Capitol. Signs read:

"Earth First!"
"No More Gods!"
"Train Us or Leave!"

What had started as awe had quickly become polarization. Some saw the Warborn as saviors, a forgotten people whose return marked a new age of strength, clarity, and destiny fulfilled. They were living myth and legend, tangible proof that the gods had not forsaken the Earth.

Others saw them as conquerors, wielders of power too great to trust, too ancient to understand, and too alien to control. And many, perhaps the most fearful of all, saw them as harbingers of the end—living omens that the final chapter of humanity had begun to write itself in blood and stars. But one truth now echoed louder than all the cries of nationalism, panic, and hope. The Svarthjarta was coming. And the time for denial had passed.

Across every continent, as if tectonic plates of ideology had shifted, new global factions formed, not along borders, but around belief.

The first faction was "The Followers of the Old Ways"

They gathered in stone temples and modern houses alike, lighting fires beside runes and prayer stones. These were the ones who embraced the Warborn. Some were Awakened themselves. Others simply believed. Led in part by charismatic Awakened such as Yrsa Bjornsdottir and Brother Malric the Skald, they taught the history of Yggdrasil, of nine realms and battles yet to come. To them, the Svarthjarta was foretold in sagas misread as myth. They built training camps, spiritual centers, and hybrid villages using Zepharian tech and Viking architecture. Their rallying cry was one of transformation through tradition:

"We were warriors once. We are again."

In the wilds of northern Sweden, a child of thirteen lifted an axe charged with light and split a tree with a single swing. Her village wept, not in fear, but in pride.

The second faction was "The Guardians of Earth"

Formed by an uneasy alliance of nations, scientific elites, and military leaders, the Guardians saw themselves as Earth's last line of measured defense. They didn't hate the Warborn. But they didn't trust them either. Their leader, General Lin Bao, had fought in orbital defense drills before the Zepharian return. He now commanded a force of over 50,000, stationed in orbital platforms and underground bastions.

"Our duty is to Earth," he often said. "Not to ancient legends or glowing bloodlines."

The Guardians monitored all Warborn activity. They intercepted communications, catalogued abilities, and pushed for containment protocols. To them, diplomacy was a shield, but readiness was the only real defense.

The final faction was "The Fearmongers"

They were scattered. Angry. Dangerous. To them, this was not a time for strategy or coexistence, it was war. Period. Conspiracy networks, rogue generals, and techno-extremist groups came together in secret bunkers and encrypted forums. They believed the Warborn were invaders, the Zepharians were colonizers, and that the Awakened were infected.

In a darkened hangar in Arizona, a prototype railgun was being assembled. Not for defense, but for assassination. They had a name for their enemy:

"The Pretender King."

They believed killing Erik Bloodaxe would shatter the Awakened and break the growing cult of Viking supremacy. They didn't realize it would only light the fuse.

In every major city, the fault lines of Earth's spiritual and political fractures deepened. While rural villages aligned themselves more swiftly, some falling back into mythic reverence, others rejecting the conflict altogether, the great cities became battlefields of ideology.

London: The Divided Parliament

In the chamber of the House of Commons, Prime Minister Abigail Trenholm stood behind a reinforced podium, her voice tight but steady.

"We cannot govern through folklore," she said. "We cannot legislate against shadows. We are a sovereign nation. We will remain one."

Half the chamber rose in applause. The other half booed and shouted.

The Warborn had taken up residency in Stonehenge, transforming the ancient site into a waypoint for energy readings and descendant awakenings. The Guardians had wanted it cordoned off. The Followers called it sacred. In between stood civilians, unsure of whether to kneel or run.

Outside the Parliament gates, protestors clashed—some wearing rune-etched cloaks, others in armor patched with the Union Jack and slogans like "Earth For Earthlings."
It wasn't just a culture war. It was a spiritual reckoning.

Tokyo: Silent Acceptance

In Japan, the government took a different path. Known for balancing ancient tradition with cutting-edge technology, the country took the Warborn's return not as chaos—but as an inevitable shift in the cosmic balance.

Temples opened to Awakened descendants. Samurai imagery merged with Norse motifs. Quiet reverence ruled the day.

One shrine in Kyoto became a place of pilgrimage and monks debated whether the runic awakenings paralleled ancient Shinto kami. Pilgrams gathered not for prayer, but for remembrance. Holographic orbs hovered in the garden, displaying visions of lost worlds, Zepharian histories, and now, Earth's possible futures.

In Lagos, crowds danced through the streets chanting the names of their ancestors, believing the Zepharians had come to test the lineage of kings. In Quebec, protesters hurled Molotovs at UN vehicles, their graffiti scrawled in Norse and French alike: "Our blood remembers."

Children bowed before depictions of Erik and Astrid as if they were kami—spiritual figures that balanced the fury of war with the weight of destiny.

Prime Minister Ishida Ren made a single, powerful statement:

"They returned. We choose not to resist change. We choose to guide it."

São Paulo: The Awakened Uprising

In Brazil, the Awakened Movement erupted into the streets. Descendants who had been hiding for months finally stepped forward. They marched openly, many demonstrating their gifts—illuminated skin, bursts of strength, runic projection. Some flew short distances through air before landing barefoot among their cheering kin. But with pride came pressure.

The president was forced into hiding after her motorcade was attacked by anti-Warborn insurgents. Vigilante groups armed with outdated alien tech began hunting Awakened in the favelas. It wasn't government policy—it was chaos.

One group, led by a war-priest named Valdo, claimed to be establishing a "Free Awakened Nation" in the Amazon basin.

"We will not ask for permission to exist," he broadcast. "We will not apologize for our birthright."

The world watched, breathless. The cities had not just split—they had begun to transform.

At the heart of Ydalir, buried beneath the carved runes and jagged cliffs, stood a subterranean command hall—Skjaldborget, the Shield Fortress. Built with the help of Zepharian engineers and Awakened stonewrights, it was more than a war room. It was a memory core, a place where past and future collided in glowing glyphs and flickering visions.

Erik Bloodaxe stood before the central projection, an interactive star map traced with pulsing lines of potential incursion paths. Around him, his inner council had assembled: each Warborn a veteran of both ancient battlefields and alien wars.

Astrid Jorgensen, now High Seer of the Waking Flame, stood to his right, cataloging Earth's Awakened population growth. Over 12,000 registered. Likely double that unregistered.

Yrsa Shieldbreaker, head of combat training, leaned against the wall, polishing her twin axes with a cloth of strange fabric that shimmered between wolf-fur and starlight.

Leif Kaarsen, a newly risen Warborn commander from Iceland, brought intelligence from the far north—glacier fractures, possible rift activity, magnetic disturbances.

And a new face had joined the circle: Dr. Malik Arden, a former UN astrophysicist turned believer. He had no runes, no bloodlink to the past, but his mind moved like fire.

"Every reading points to a singularity forming near the Martian orbit," Malik said, pacing. "It's not stable. It's collapsing and expanding and oscillating. And something is trying to come through."

"What kind of something?" Yrsa asked, tossing her cloth aside.

"Something... coordinated," Malik replied. "We've seen this pattern in the data before, on Lerna IX. Right before it vanished."

Erik nodded slowly. "A testing rift."

Astrid's pulse quickened. "So they're probing our system."

"They're hunting," Malik corrected. "Testing resonance. Measuring what it can pull through."

Erik turned to the group. "We hold the high ground for now. Earth is fortified. But we cannot hold it alone."

Leif frowned. "The Guardians will never ally with us. And Earth's armies barely speak to each other, let alone train together."

"They will," Astrid said quietly. "Or they'll be dust."

The Warborn had begun implementing three simultaneous strategies:

Shield Mobilization — A planetary lattice of runic energy fields augmented by Zepharian technology. It would not block the Svarthjarta, but it might slow their entry long enough to mount a defense.

Memory Recovery — Scattered across Earth were lost Zepharian archives, buried during the Warborn's exodus. These relics contained forgotten techniques, tactics, and weapons. Awakened scout teams were dispatched to track them.

Ritual Synthesis — A fusion of Norse invocation rites and Zepharian frequency resonance. If mastered, this might allow the Awakened to project fields of willforce—protective energies bound not by physics but by belief.

But there was a fourth initiative, known only to Erik and Astrid. It was called: The Last Flame. And it could not be used unless all else failed.

Even among the Awakened, unity frayed. The Warborn had returned as symbols, legends reborn, walking myths. But not all who carried runes agreed on what came next. With power came fear, ambition, and uncertainty. And beneath the disciplined hierarchy of the Warborn, something volatile was beginning to simmer.

Soren Blackhand, once a loyal trainee, had risen swiftly. Too swiftly. His runes burned black, an anomaly never seen among other Awakened. He claimed they were drawn from ancestral battlefields, from souls who had refused to pass into Valhalla. Others whispered darker things—that he had touched a fragment of the Svarthjarta in a dream and survived.

"Why should we wait for the end to find us?" Soren demanded one night during a training council. "Why should we react when we could strike first?"

He stood before a gathering of twenty elite Awakened, all handpicked from various factions. Some were curious. Others silent. A few looked to each other uneasily.

Yrsa had warned Astrid about Soren weeks ago. "He doesn't fight to protect," she had said. "He fights to rule."

Now that warning rang in Astrid's ears as word reached her that Soren had established a breakaway faction called The Forged, warriors who trained in secret, using enhanced rituals and weaponry not approved by the Warborn council.

They had taken up residence in a former underground Zepharian testing complex beneath the Scottish Highlands. Sealed off from Ydalir's command structure. Isolated. Dangerous.

She went alone. Against Erik's recommendation. Against Yrsa's wishes. Inside the Zepharian vault, Soren waited.

"You shouldn't have come alone," he said, voice echoing off the metallic walls.

Astrid didn't flinch. "You've built a cult, not a command."

Soren approached slowly, runes glowing along his jawline like cracks in obsidian.

"We're the ones who see the truth," he said. "The old ways are chains. The gods? Dead. What remains is evolution. Purpose. Fire."

"And what about loyalty?" she snapped. "To your people. To the world we're trying to save?"

"I am loyal," he said. "To power. To survival. And if that means building a new order from the ashes of the old, so be it."

"You'd burn the world to prove yourself."

Soren stepped closer, their eyes inches apart. "Only if it means it survives."

Astrid didn't strike him. She didn't draw her blade. But when she returned to Ydalir, she locked down the Forged's access. And in her report to Erik, she wrote one sentence:

"We may face more than one enemy when the sky breaks."

It began with a vibration no one could hear. Above the Atlantic, the clouds churned unnaturally, spiraling outward like the eye of a cosmic storm. Commercial planes were rerouted. Satellites flickered. Tides shifted centimeters, then meters. Then meters more. And then came the sound.

A deep, resonant hum, sub-audible, yet felt in every chest cavity. Dogs howled. Birds scattered. Machines hiccupped. Children stopped speaking mid-sentence.

In a naval command center off the coast of Greenland, a technician shouted:

"There's a rupture forming. Thirty klicks wide and growing!"

The rift tore open like a wound in the heavens. No fire. No explosion. Just absence. A hole through which nothing bled. Within it: shapes. Unclear. Twisting. As if the void had bones.

From Skjaldborget, Erik watched in silence. Astrid stood beside him, her fists clenched, eyes wide.

"It's early," she whispered. "We thought we had weeks."

"Time is the first casualty of war," Erik replied.

He activated the alarm. Deep horns howled across Ydalir. Zepharian shields snapped to full charge. Awakened teams scrambled into position—shieldmaidens with light-etched armor, berserkers chanting ancient oaths, Warborn readying weapons that pulsed with the blood of stars.

But Earth was not ready.

From the rift, a single entity slipped through. It moved like fog and flame. Its edges never resolved—a creature made of hunger, its shape shifting between limbs, tendrils, and mouths. Eyes blinked open and closed across its form, each one blacker than void, gazing into dimensions that shouldn't exist. It shrieked—not with sound, but with memory.

People across the planet collapsed into seizures, visions flooding their minds of places long devoured, of civilizations lost to teeth that never closed.

Erik Bloodaxe stepped through a portal above Greenland, his axe blazing with radiant energy. Around him, twenty

Warborn descended in formation. The sky cracked as they struck. Steel and light clashed with darkness and despair. Zepharian disruptor beams sliced through tendrils. Runic shields shattered on impact, reforged seconds later through battle-screamed oaths.

The Svarthjarta beast fought like a storm without direction, lashing out, spreading itself thinner with each strike. But the Warborn did not falter.

Astrid's voice echoed in every Awakened's mind through the battle mesh.

"For Earth. For blood. For the forgotten flame."

In twenty minutes, the creature collapsed into itself, ragged screaming back into the void. The rift sealed behind it. The silence that followed was deafening.

Across the world, people stared at the sky. Some wept. Some prayed. Some simply stood still. The war had not come. It had begun.

The Zepharians said little. Observed much. Some claimed they only appeared to those who had already changed. Others whispered that they were choosing sides—not in politics, but in bloodlines.

Back at Ydalir, Erik removed his helmet. His beard was soaked with sweat, and blood trickled from a gash across his forehead. He looked at Astrid, voice low but certain.

"This was the first. The others... are already watching."

She nodded, her jaw set.

"Then we teach them how to fear us."

Chapter 10: Identity Crisis

The world was fracturing. The return of the Warborn, the awakening of the Descendants, and the looming shadow of the Svarthjarta had created a reality where the past, present, and future were colliding in a war that no one truly understood.

For those of Norse descent, the battle was not just external, it was a war within themselves. Were they still human? Or were they something more? The question hung over every Descendant like a curse and a crown.

Dr. Astrid Jorgensen had spent her life as a scientist, a historian, a seeker of knowledge. She had walked ancient battlefields in silence, run her fingers across stones etched with forgotten runes, and written academic papers questioning the supernatural while secretly longing to believe in it. Her identity had always been firmly rooted in the known, the provable.

But ever since the day she had seen the first visions, since the moment she had looked in the mirror and found the runic markings glowing on her skin, she had begun to question everything. She was no longer just Astrid Jorgensen. She was something else. And she didn't know who she was becoming.

Every night, the dreams came, not just of the past, but of what was to come. The visions were no longer fleeting flickers of strange imagery. They had become entire experiences: overwhelming, immersive, terrifying.
She saw herself standing on a battlefield unlike anything in Earth's history, clad in armor forged from starlight and steel, its surface reflecting constellations that had no names in any Earthly tongue. Her hands held a weapon that pulsed with both ancient Norse magic and alien technology, its edge crackling with energy. She saw herself leading warriors into battle, not against men, but against shadows that moved

like living nightmares, creatures with a thousand eyes and no soul. And in every dream, she heard the same voice—deep, ethereal, and ancient:

"You must choose, Astrid." You cannot be both. You are either Viking… or nothing at all."

That voice haunted her waking hours as much as her sleep.

She tried to rationalize it. Tried to tell herself that it was stress, that it was psychosomatic, that the body under enough strain could play tricks on the mind. But deep down, she knew better. The runes on her arms didn't lie. Nor did the enhanced hearing, the moments of prescient awareness, or the time she instinctively caught a falling scalpel between two fingers before it even hit the floor. She'd stopped talking to the government handlers. They didn't understand. How could they? Men in suits didn't dream of Ragnarok or hear Odin's call. They wanted data, charts, and blood samples. Not prophecy.

And so Astrid spent most of her days alone, in the Arctic base where the Drakenskip had been excavated. She would sit on the ancient deck and feel the low thrum of the ship under her palms. She no longer questioned how it was still alive. The ship knew her. It remembered her. And that scared her more than anything.

On a bitterly cold evening, wrapped in her fur-lined coat, Astrid stood beside the ship, her breath curling like smoke into the night air. The auroras above painted the sky in streaks of emerald and violet, pulsing in rhythm with her own heartbeat.

A sound, too quiet for normal ears, made her turn. From the shadows, a figure emerged. One of the Warborn.

He was taller than most men, his eyes glowing faintly beneath the wolf-helm that crowned his brow. His armor shimmered with both alien alloy and etched Norse designs. He looked both futuristic and ancient, a contradiction made flesh.

"You've come," Astrid said, her voice low. "I need answers."

The Warborn nodded solemnly. "Then you are ready to hear them."

She stepped closer, trying not to flinch at the heat rolling off his body. "Why is this happening to me? To all of us? What are we becoming?"

The Warborn studied her in silence. When he finally spoke, his voice was gravel wrapped in thunder.

"You are not becoming anything," he said. "You are remembering."

"Remembering?" she echoed.

"You were never only human. Not fully. You are the continuation of a bloodline born in fire and ice, tempered in battle, and carried through the stars."

He paused and gestured to the ship behind her.

"The Zepharians did not create you. They awakened you. You are what your ancestors always meant you to be."

Astrid swallowed, the weight of his words hitting her like a blow.

"And if I don't want it? If I want to go back to the way things were?"

The Warborn's eyes darkened.

"Then you will be the first to die when the Black Heart arrives."

A chill ran down her spine that had nothing to do with the Arctic wind.

The Warborn's words lingered in Astrid's mind long after he had vanished into the snow-shrouded night.

"Then you will be the first to die when the Black Heart arrives."

It wasn't a threat. It wasn't even anger. It was a statement of fact, like telling someone the sun would rise, or that fire burns. But for Astrid, it lit a different fire. Not one of panic, but one of defiance. She would not die a symbol. She would not be consumed as an unfinished weapon. She would understand what she was becoming.

Astrid was not the only one struggling. All over the world, descendants were awakening, their abilities growing stronger with each passing day. Some embraced their newfound power. Others feared it. But the rest of the world? The rest of the world saw them as a threat.

Governments began tracking those who carried Norse DNA, forcing them into containment facilities, attempting to understand and control what was happening.
But the descendants were not meant to be controlled.
And when the first resistance movements began, the war between humanity and its own future truly began.

In cities across the globe, things were unraveling. The Awakened, once seen with curiosity or reverence, were now being hunted in some regions.

In Germany, a radical group called Purity Pact raided a village of Awakened farmers in the Black Forest. Fires were lit. Families were dragged into the streets. Cameras captured grainy footage of a Descendant shielding a child with his body as drones fired stun rounds at his chest. He didn't fall. The footage went viral.

In South Africa, a young Awakened healer was killed by police during a misunderstanding in Johannesburg. The crowd turned violent. The city burned for two days.

And in Alberta, Canada, a peaceful demonstration ended in a massacre when private contractors working for an anti-Warborn syndicate opened fire with prototype magnetic rifles designed specifically to pierce runic shields.
The world was splitting, not by geography, but by evolution.
The Old Human Order versus the New Blood Rising.

Astrid watched as the first execution took place. The Guardians of Earth, those who sought to rid the world of the Viking bloodline, had captured one of the strongest descendants, a man named Sigurd Halvorsen, who had once been nothing more than a fisherman in Denmark.

But after the awakening? His strength had tripled. His reflexes had become superhuman. He had stopped a bullet with his bare hand. And for that, the world saw him as a monster. They put him in chains. They called him a danger to humanity. And then, in front of the entire world...They executed him. Not because of what he had done. But because of what he was becoming.

Astrid felt rage boil inside her, the same rage that was spreading like wildfire through the Descendants.

"They will kill us all," one of them said. "Unless we fight back."

And for the first time, Astrid did not disagree.

The next morning, Astrid made her way to one of the
Zepharian sanctums carved into the glacier cliffs
surrounding Ydalir. It was said to be a place of resonance,
where the interface between mind and memory could be
controlled, even expanded.

Yrsa met her there.

"I heard about your conversation," Yrsa said without
greeting. "He shouldn't have said it that way."

"But he's right, isn't he?" Astrid said.

Yrsa studied her for a moment, arms crossed, her cloak
swirling in the cold.

"You're a bridge, Astrid. Between Earth and sky. Between
logic and faith. But you don't have to walk across all at
once."

Astrid nodded but stepped into the sanctum anyway.
The chamber inside was pulsing faintly with ambient
Zepharian energy with columns of light rising and falling like
breath. At the center was a ring of runes embedded into the
stone floor.

"This is called the Stone of Svarilaug," Yrsa explained. "It
shows you what you fear, not to punish you, but to see if
you can command it."

Astrid stepped into the circle without hesitation. The light
dimmed. And then the world unraveled.

She was no longer standing in Ydalir. She was standing in the
heart of a ruined city, glass towers melted, skies torn by
gravitational fractures, and bodies strewn across blackened

streets. Not just humans, Warborn too. Dead. Torn apart. Their runes dark. Above her, a gash in the sky spilled ink into reality. The Svarthjarta had come. And Earth had fallen.

A figure approached her across the rubble, herself, but different. This version of Astrid was clad in blood-red armor, her eyes glowing not with Zepharian light, but with the oily shimmer of the Black Heart. Her runes twisted across her arms like shackles.

"You hesitated," the dark Astrid said. "You held onto your science. You clung to humanity. And you broke us."

The ground cracked beneath Astrid's feet. Flames rose. She fell—

—and gasped awake inside the sanctum, drenched in sweat, her legs trembling.

Yrsa knelt beside her. "You saw it?"

Astrid nodded, too breathless to speak.

Yrsa helped her up. "Good. Now we know what we're fighting for."

Astrid stood before the council of Warborn that night, her robe streaked with ash from the sanctum's visions, her voice stripped of hesitation.

"I am no longer uncertain," she said. "I am no longer afraid of what I am becoming."

Erik watched her silently, nodding once.

"We cannot delay the gathering of the Twelve," she continued. "The Circle of Flame must be lit. If we wait, the world will burn before we even lift a sword."

Yrsa raised an eyebrow. "Even the Forged?"

Astrid exhaled. "Even Soren. We don't have the luxury of division."

Erik stood, his presence dimming the very light in the chamber.

"Then prepare the rites. And prepare yourself."

He stepped closer, placing a hand on her shoulder.

"Because the next time you face yourself," he said softly, "it won't be a vision. It will be war."

The night the Twelve gathered, the stars hid behind clouds. Inside the Hall of Wyrd, deep beneath the frozen crust of Ydalir, the walls pulsed with runic light. The room had no ceiling, only an open shaft leading straight into the sky. It was said that in the earliest days, the gods had thrown their voices through that shaft like lightning through a spear.
Now it served a new purpose.

Astrid stood in the center of the ring, a circle carved from obsidian and rimmed with twelve distinct stones, each inscribed with the ancient mark of a lineage lost to time. This was the Circle of Flame, not a literal fire, but a binding of purpose. It was the oath of unity spoken by Warborn chieftains in the last cycle before their disappearance.
And now, for the first time in a thousand years, it would be lit again.

One by one, they came.

Yrsa Shieldbreaker, the strongest of them, placed her hand on the red stone of strength, flames licking her palm.

Leif Kaarsen, scholar and strategist, laid his touch on the blue stone of wisdom.

Thorn Alriksson, former assassin turned guardian, claimed the black stone of shadow.

Runa the Silent, a seer from the Far North whose eyes never closed, placed her palm on the green stone of vision.

Others followed—Descendants from Kenya, Mongolia, Chile, and Siberia. The runes had spread farther than anyone had imagined. Some bore names written in no known language, their ancestors erased from history by time and war. Yet they stood now, awakened by blood, by fate, by memory. And finally, Astrid.

She placed her hand upon the central stone, the White Flame, the one that had no name. It was the place of convergence. The flame that bound the others. As her hand met the stone, a low hum echoed through the hall. The lights above flared. The runes lit as one. The Circle of Flame was complete.

Erik Bloodaxe stepped into the ring once the flame stabilized. His armor was adorned not for battle, but for ceremony, dark and regal, with fur draped across his shoulders and a wolf-skull crown. He raised a heavy torch of pale fire and spoke in Old Norse.

"Veien er mørk. Skyggene kaller. Vi svarer ikke med bønn, men med flamme."

Astrid translated aloud for the younger Awakened in the room.

"The path is dark. The shadows call. We do not answer with prayer, but with flame."

Erik turned to the Twelve.

"One day soon, Earth will not be enough. The Svarthjarta does not take planets. It takes systems. It devours meaning. And we—" he slammed the torch into the circle "—are meaning made manifest."

Each of the Twelve repeated a single phrase in turn.

"We are the fire that answers silence."

The ceremony was barely over when an unexpected alarm crackled through the sanctum. Astrid turned, her senses already racing. Yrsa drew a weapon. Runa tilted her head.

A portal bloomed in the center of the chamber, glimmering not with gold or blue, but a faint violet. Something unstable. Unwelcomed. And from it stepped Soren Blackhand. He wore no armor. No weapons. His hands were open. But the runes on his body glowed black, faintly veined with silver. His eyes pulsed with residual energy, like a dying star refusing to collapse.

Astrid stepped forward. "You weren't invited."

Soren smiled without warmth. "I came anyway."

Yrsa reached for her axe. "We don't need your kind here."

But Erik raised a hand. "Let him speak."

Soren's smile widened. "You're gathering unity, forging symbols, lighting fires in the dark. That's noble. But it won't be enough."

He stepped into the Circle of Flame without permission. The runes did not reject him, but flickered, confused.

"I have seen what comes through the next rift," Soren said.

"Not the scouts. Not the beast you fought over Greenland. I've seen the generals. The singers of oblivion."

The hall fell silent.

"You want to hold a line," Soren continued. "I want to rewrite the battlefield."

Astrid stared at him, something stirring behind her eyes.

"You want to burn down the world to save it."

"I want to replace it."

Erik stepped forward, close now. "And if you force our hand?"

Soren's eyes glinted. "Then I'll remind you how dangerous a mirror can be."

And he vanished, leaving behind only echoes.

In the wake of Soren's sudden departure, the chamber remained still. The Circle of Flame flickered uneasily, its cohesion rattled by his intrusion. Some of the Twelve muttered prayers under their breath; others reached instinctively for their weapons. None dared speak too soon.

Astrid felt the cold return, not from the air, but from within. A chill that began where certainty once lived.

Yrsa broke the silence first. "He shouldn't have been able to stand in the Circle. It should've burned him."

Erik's face was stone. "The Circle doesn't burn lies. It burns division. Soren is not divided. He believes what he says."

"Which is exactly what makes him dangerous," Astrid murmured.

Later that night, in the upper chamber of Ydalir, Astrid sat with Leif Kaarsen and Runa, the three of them gathered around a holographic projection of Earth's leyline grids and Zepharian beacon pulses. Threads of luminous data wove through the map, highlighting stress points where Svarthjarta energies were most likely to pierce. But it wasn't the map that consumed Astrid's mind. It was the memory of Soren's face, confident, calm, sure. Too sure.

"Did we miscalculate?" she asked. "Are we pushing our people into something they're not ready for?"

Leif looked at her from over his spectacles, brushing a speck of ash off his coat. "We're not pushing them. We're showing them where to stand."

"But we're not united," she countered. "And unity isn't optional anymore."

Runa, eyes always half-lidded, reached across the table and placed a hand on Astrid's. "Unity does not mean sameness. It means clarity. You know your path. Walk it. They'll follow."

Astrid exhaled. And in that moment, she understood. She would not wait for consensus. She would lead.

The next day, Astrid stood before the central Zepharian beacon tower, a structure of translucent alloy that rose like a needle through the Arctic sky. Around her, technicians calibrated signal bursts while Zepharian sentinels stood motionless, their forms casting thin shadows over the snow. A drone activated. The beacon pulsed.

And across the globe, a signal was transmitted, not encoded, not political. Spoken plainly, in the voice of a woman caught between worlds.

"My name is Astrid Jorgensen. I was born of Earth, but I carry the blood of stars. The world is changing. So are we. This is not about alien invasion. This is not about religion, or race, or governments. This is about survival. The Svarthjarta is coming. You've seen the signs. It will not negotiate. It will not stop. And yet, we stand. We are the Warborn. We remember what your ancestors forgot. And if we must stand alone, we will still hold the line."

The signal ended.

Within hours, the sky screamed again. This time above the Pacific. Satellites shattered from the blast. Ships capsized from the pulse. Islands darkened. But something was different. The rift wasn't leaking shadow. It was breathing light.

Golden tendrils arced across the sky like auroras laced with electricity, and from them descended five shapes, tall, robed, glowing. Not Zepharians. Not Warborn. Something else.

Yrsa watched the projections in the war room. "New players."

Leif nodded. "New rules."

Astrid turned toward Erik.

His eyes remained fixed on the screen. "Then we speak with them."

"And if they're not here to talk?" she asked.

Erik gripped the hilt of his axe.

"Then we'll remind them what the Warborn are."

That night, Astrid walked alone to the peak of Ydalir. The stars had returned. Clear, sharp, endless. She looked upward and whispered:

"Who am I now?"

And the wind answered. Not in words, but in fire. Behind her, the Circle of Flame still burned, unchallenged, unbroken. For now. But she knew the war had just begun.

Chapter 11: Unveiling the Truth

The storm had not yet broken, but the world knew it was coming. Above Ydalir, dark clouds churned in uneasy silence. The auroras no longer danced. They hung like ghost-lights, frozen in the sky. The ground beneath the valley pulsed with unseen energy as if the very bones of the Earth were preparing for something sacred, or catastrophic.

Inside the great ceremonial circle of Skjaldborget, carved from ancient stone and ringed by Zepharian alloy pillars, Erik Bloodaxe stood at the center, not to be revealed, but to be reaffirmed.

For centuries, Erik Bloodaxe had been a legend, a figure of history, a name spoken in myth and song. But now, he stood before them, not as a memory, not as a spirit, but as a man. Alive. Unchanged. His armor gleamed in the dim light of the storm-wracked sky, a fusion of Viking steel and alien craftsmanship, the runes etched into his breastplate glowing with an otherworldly fire.

He had returned months ago, his reappearance shaking the foundation of history and myth alike. Since then, he had led, fought, bled, and burned beside the Awakened. He had built alliances, trained armies, and held the line against the creeping dark of the Svarthjarta. But tonight was different.

Tonight, the Warborn would bind themselves to him, not just as comrades, but as a converged force, warriors of Earth and stars alike. They called it the Ceremony of Binding.

The wind howled through the pillars as the Warborn gathered in their finest ceremonial garb. Furs woven with threads of starlight. Armor etched with glowing runes. Every generation of the awakened stood present, from the elder shieldmaidens who had trained beside Erik in forgotten moons, to young Descendants who had awakened only weeks ago, their powers raw and untested.

Hakon Stormcaller stepped forward first. Once Erik's second in command during the exodus, he now led the Western Warborn Legion, headquartered near Greenland's eastern range.He knelt, not in surrender, not in worship, but in ancient tradition.

"We kneel, not to a king of blood," Hakon said, "but to the fire that leads us through the dark."

One by one, the Warborn followed. The kneeling was not enforced. It was chosen.

Astrid Jorgensen stood beside Yrsa Shieldbreaker and Leif Kaarsen, her eyes on Erik, her heart pounding. She had come so far from the halls of academia, from cold university floors and chalk-dusted rune tables. She had been reborn not by accident, but by necessity. And now, she was more than a scholar. She was a symbol of what the Warborn could become, past and future, knowledge and power, mind and flame.

Yrsa leaned in. "He hates this part," she whispered with a grin.

"The kneeling?" Astrid murmured.

"No. The speeches."

Erik, hearing them, allowed a rare half-smile before his face grew solemn again. He stepped forward, unsheathing the ceremonial sword Skornyr, the Blade of Remembrance, its edge glowing with a pale light that pulsed with each word spoken.

"I ask no one to kneel who does not remember," he said, his voice low but carrying. "I claim no throne forged in blood. I demand no allegiance born of fear. But if you would stand with me... then stand truly."

A ripple passed through the Warborn. Some rose. Some remained kneeling. All placed a hand over their chest, their runes glowing in unison. The ground pulsed. The pillars sang. The Binding was complete.

Though the ceremony was sacred and held in the heart of Ydalir, it was not secret. Dozens of governments and powers had been invited to observe, their representatives seated in the raised stone amphitheater surrounding the circle.

President Trenholm of the United Kingdom sat wrapped in her navy overcoat, flanked by security agents. Her expression was unreadable.

Prime Minister Ishida of Japan watched silently, murmuring into a translation earbud, his eyes fixed on Astrid more than Erik.

General Lin Bao, now head of Earth's Defense Network, stood with arms crossed, gaze sharp and skeptical.

Even Dr. Malik Arden, former UN astrophysicist, now ambassador to the Warborn, was present. He recorded the ritual with a compact holographic slate, noting the precise moments the pillar frequencies aligned with Zepharian energy pulses. Some were moved. Some were disturbed. But none could deny that something was changing.

When the ceremony concluded, Erik remained still in the circle, looking upward.

"How long?" he asked quietly.

Astrid approached. She already knew what he meant.

"Less than a week," she said. "The second stable rift is forming near the lunar corridor."

Leif joined them, opening a hologram. "Energy readings show a pattern, three pulses, equidistant. It's the same frequency we picked up before the Pacific incident."

Yrsa tightened her jaw. "Which means another one is coming."

Hakon stepped beside Erik.

"And this one won't be a scout."

"No," Erik agreed. "This one will speak. Or strike."

Later that night, as the wind died and the sky cleared, Astrid returned to the Circle alone. She touched one of the still-glowing stones, feeling its hum beneath her fingertips. She thought of the generations to come. Of her ancestors. Of the blood in her veins. Of the storm to come. She didn't kneel. She didn't pray. She stood. Because the time for questions had passed. The war ahead would not be for territory or pride. It would be for history itself.

The Binding had ended. The echoes of solemn oaths still lingered in the air, but already, the mood in Ydalir had shifted. There was no time for celebration. No feast. No songs. Not yet. The world was watching, and some eyes no longer saw allies. They saw targets.

Inside the high command chamber, the temperature dropped several degrees as Erik entered. He moved with the presence of a seasoned warlord, but now, his movements were measured and calculated. He was no longer leading raiders. He was leading a planet.

At the oval war table stood representatives from Earth's major blocs: The Earth Defense Coalition (EDC), the League of the Awakened, and the Zepharian Liaison Corps. General Lin Bao was the first to speak.

"Ceremony or not, we still don't have alignment from half the governments in the Americas, most of Africa, or anything from the Moscow Compact. Binding rituals mean little to those without runes, Lord Erik."

He didn't spit the title, but it dripped skepticism all the same. Erik met the general's eyes without blinking.

"I do not need their loyalty. I need their cooperation."

"You'll have neither," Lin replied. "Not if we can't promise them containment."

Astrid stepped forward. "Containment is not an option anymore. The Svarthjarta's next arrival isn't a theory, it's a mathematical certainty. Our best defense is preparation, not secrecy."

Lin leaned in. "And what about the Forged?"

The chamber hushed.

"They're building weaponry we don't understand. Training Awakened without oversight. And their last transmission came from near one of the old Zepharian grave-sites. That's not a coincidence."

The Forged. Soren's faction. Once just a fringe rebellion of strong-willed Awakened, now they were a rising power unto themselves. And they were growing fast.

Using unsanctioned rituals, Zepharian relics, and untested rites of awakening, Soren had accelerated the development of his warriors. They weren't just stronger. They were... different.

The last intel brief showed one of his warriors phase-shifting through stone walls. Another turned kinetic force into concussive runic bursts. None of that was part of the core Warborn rites. Some of it wasn't even Zepharian.

Erik rubbed a hand over his beard.

"Soren wants to fight the Svarthjarta his way. That's dangerous. But if he succeeds… it could also save us."

Yrsa, leaning against the far wall, growled. "Or destroy everything we've tried to build."

"Then we find out which," Astrid said. "Before the next rift opens."

As if summoned by the words, the holographic table flickered. A new Zepharian AI node activated, streaming data pulses in tight bursts.

Leif translated on the fly. "Signal burst from the lunar observation ring. We've got rift-fluctuation… and transmission fragments."

He tapped a series of keys. The room filled with a broken audio signature,like metal grinding inside wind, layered over what sounded like a distorted chant.

Astrid's breath caught.

"I've heard this before," she said. "In the sanctum. During my test."

"What does it say?" asked Lin.

She paused. Then repeated the fragmented syllables, her voice shifting into a whisper of half-forgotten prophecy.

"The Heart Awaits the Hollow. The Flame Betrays Itself.
Memory Must Burn… To Awaken the Devourer."

The room fell into stillness. Even the Zepharian observers
exchanged subtle gestures of alarm.

"That's not a threat," Astrid said. "It's a ritual. A warning. Or
maybe… an invitation."

Erik nodded once. "We're running out of time."

Three days later, the Council of Earth Unity, a hastily formed
coalition between aligned governments, fractured live on
broadcast. A bomb detonated in Geneva, just blocks from
the summit center.

The target: Ambassador Nyala DuPont, an Awakened
diplomat from Senegal advocating for Zepharian technology
to be shared globally. She survived. Four civilians didn't.
The attack was claimed by a radical humanist group calling
itself Veilfire.

Their manifesto was simple:

"The skies do not belong to gods, nor to bloodlines. Earth is
for Earth."

In retaliation, Awakened militias in Berlin torched a Veilfire
recruiting house, killing eleven. Overnight, protests spread
in both directions, calls for Awakened registration, cries for
total militarization, and escalating whispers that Soren's way
might not be so wrong after all. In private, some whispered
what none dared say aloud:

"What if we need a monster to face one?"

Erik called a closed meeting in the Hall of Wyrd. Only the Twelve. Only the trusted.

"We need to send someone into the next rift."

The words landed like thunder.

Leif stood up. "No one's returned from a Svarthjarta rift, not even probes."

"I didn't say return," Erik said. "I said go."

Astrid didn't flinch. "I'll do it."

Yrsa was on her feet in an instant. "Like Hel you will."

But Astrid's voice was calm. "I've already touched their shadow. I've felt the edges of what they are. I'm the only one who's seen the inside and survived it."

Erik met her eyes. "I need a window, Astrid. Not a grave."

"You'll have both," she said. "If we wait."

The chamber known as the Ljóshlið, or "Edge of Light," had not been used since the original exodus of the Warborn. Hollowed from a singular crystalline Zepharian mineral, the interior shimmered like starlight trapped in ice. Energy pooled in streams across the floor, running like veins beneath Astrid's feet.

This was where rift entries were launched. And where few had ever returned.

Astrid stood at the center of the chamber, her armor unlike anything she'd ever worn before. It had been forged over the last forty-eight hours by both Warborn metallurgists and

Zepharian engineers—a fusion of the physical and metaphysical.

The plating was layered with memory-bonded alloy, woven between living runes that adjusted based on her neural impulses. She carried no weapon in the traditional sense. Instead, she wore a bracer called the Hjartablóð, or Heartblood, capable of channeling both her internal rune energy and Zepharian harmonic signatures.

Her mind felt clear. Focused. Not fearless,but resolved. This wasn't a mission. This was a crossing. A trial of flame and memory.

Before the breach, those closest to her arrived one by one. Yrsa was first. She embraced Astrid without words, squeezing her hard enough to crack ribs. Her voice, when it finally came, was low and ragged.

"Come back. Or I'll tear that rift apart myself."

Astrid smiled. "You'd probably win."

Next came Leif, awkward as ever, carrying a pouch of shimmering dust.

"Dream ash," he said, avoiding her eyes. "If your consciousness fragments, this might help you hold shape." She accepted it wordlessly. The weight of his worry made her heart heavier than the armor.

Runa came last, silent, pressing a coin of obsidian into Astrid's palm. The seer's breath touched her ear.

"When the world forgets you, this will not."

And then, at last, Erik entered. The others left. He said nothing at first, only looked at her. His eyes, which had seen stars die and warriors fall, softened.

"You don't have to do this."

Astrid stepped forward. "Yes. I do."

"You've already proven yourself."

"It's not about proving anything. It's about understanding."

She reached up, gently touching his bearded cheek.

"If I don't come back, don't let them fall apart."

Erik's jaw clenched. He leaned his forehead against hers for a long, breathless moment. Then stepped away. And nodded.

As she stepped into the core of Ljóshlið, the chamber dimmed. Zepharian monoliths aligned in concentric rings above and below her. The runes in her bracer pulsed in time with the energy convergence. Astrid focused on her breath, letting her heart slow, syncing her rhythm with the machinery.

"Initiating fold breach," said the AI calmly.

"No rescue signal," Leif's voice echoed through the comm. "We'll track you as far as we can."

"We're with you," added Yrsa.

The world began to hum. Not in noise, but in gravity. Reality folded like paper around her. Shapes twisted. Light turned to language. Color fragmented into taste. And then—

A flash. A sound like her own name whispered by a thousand versions of herself. And everything went dark.

There was no up. No down. No here. Astrid floated through a storm of memory. Not hers. Not anyone's. All. She saw cities that had never existed, and oceans made of sound. Stars blinked in and out like thoughts.

And then—shapes. Not creatures. Not machines. Concepts. One approached her. Its form was... readable. Not in body, but in intention. It pressed against her mind.

"Flame. Seeker. Blood-marked."

She spoke, though her mouth did not move.

"Who are you?"

"We are what burns the sky. What waits beneath names. What remembers nothing and wants to make you the same."

"Svarthjarta."

"You named us. We devour names."

Pain lanced through her head. Her runes flared, trying to anchor her.

"Why come now?" she asked.

"Because you lit the fire. Because you seek. Because he has returned."

"Erik?"

"The breaker. The blade. The end."

The pressure increased. Astrid's armor cracked. Her bracer sparked. Images burned across her vision: Soren standing on a broken Earth, flames rising from the sky. Warborn dead. Erik surrounded by voidlight.

"You will remember nothing when we are done."
She screamed—

—and light exploded.

She felt herself torn backward, ripped from the void by an unseen tether.

Astrid collapsed into the Ljóshlið with a soundless scream. Her body convulsed. The armor was cracked and steaming. Her eyes rolled back. The chamber lights surged. Erik was the first to reach her, catching her just as her legs gave out.

"She's burning," Yrsa shouted, kneeling beside them.

"No," Erik said. "She's remembering."

The medical sanctum beneath Ydalir had never held a patient like Astrid. She lay still for two days, her vitals erratic, brain activity peaking at levels the Zepharian monitors had no frame of reference for. Neural storms flickered through the holographic projections around her, her mind simultaneously active and fragmented, as though it were replaying every memory she had ever known, and some she had never lived.

Yrsa paced the corridor like a caged wolf, pausing only to check with the medics before resuming her circuit.

Leif sat nearby, reviewing Rift telemetry again and again, whispering to himself.

"Three layers of dimensional bleed… quantum displacement… she should be dead."

And yet, she breathed.

The medical sanctum beneath Ydalir buzzed with quiet urgency. Astrid Jorgensen's body remained still, but her mind, according to every Zepharian diagnostic, was hyperactive, overclocked. Her neural activity danced at frequencies only theoretical in human biology. Her mind wasn't dreaming. It wasn't hallucinating. It was translating something. Not language. Not memory. Possibility.

Yrsa stood guard in the hallway like a storm contained in armor. Leif paced, surrounded by screens and runic charts. Runa meditated in a trance, her mouth silently forming words no one could hear. Everyone was waiting for Astrid to wake. But the truth was, she was already elsewhere.

She woke on the third night. No sudden gasp. No spasms. Just a breath, slow, calm, knowing. Her eyes opened. Not wide, but with a steadiness that froze Erik in place as he stepped into the room. Silver fire ringed her irises now. Not Zepharian or Warborn but something new.

She sat up slowly. Her armor, cracked from reentry, pulsed faintly where the Hjartablóð bracer fused to her skin. It had bled light and sealed over her wrist like a brand. Erik was by her side before she could swing her legs off the bed.

"You were gone for almost seventy-two hours," Erik said.

"No," she whispered. "I was ahead."

Yrsa and Leif entered quickly, their faces hard with concern. Astrid closed her eyes and whispered:

"I saw what waits beyond the veil. Not just the Svarthjarta. Not just destruction. I saw... what it feeds on."

Later, in the high chamber beneath the skyvault, she stood before the inner circle—Erik, Yrsa, Leif, Runa, Hakon—and told them what she had seen.

"The Svarthjarta is not a swarm. It's not a hunger in the way we understand it. It doesn't come to erase the past. It doesn't fear our history. It feeds on the one thing more dangerous than war or fire."

She met each of their gazes in turn.

"It feeds on potential."

Leif tilted his head, puzzled. "Like what we might become?"

Astrid nodded.

"It tracks civilizations nearing a moment of transformation, species on the edge of evolution, consciousness that's about to awaken, technology at the tipping point of transcendence. It doesn't kill what is. It kills what could be."

Yrsa exhaled slowly.

"That's why it came now. Why it didn't strike during the Black Death. Or the World Wars. Because we weren't ready then."

"But we are now," Erik said. "The Warborn, the Descendants, the alliances. We've lit a fire, and it saw the smoke."

Astrid turned toward the artifact that Leif had retrieved during her absence, a spear-shaped core of fused alloy and rune-crystal.

"That's the Eidrsigil," Leif explained. "It was meant to preserve identity. But it might be more than that."

She placed her hand on it. Felt it respond.

"It's not a memory-keeper. It's a seed. A beacon of potential energy, unrealized futures stored in a single point. That's what the Svarthjarta fears. And hungers for."

She closed her eyes.

"We can use it. If we plant it inside the rift, it might force the Svarthjarta to manifest, a physical anchor. Give us a battlefield. Something we can hit."

Hakon leaned on the table. "And if it doesn't?"

"Then it consumes us before we get the chance to become who we're meant to be."

At dawn, the sky broke again. The rift that formed above Earth was unlike the others, stable, deliberate. A corridor of coalescing light and shadows, rotating like a spiral galaxy collapsing into a tunnel.

Signals began to stream through Earth's satellites, geometry encoded in pulses, recursive patterns resonating with Awakened DNA. The Svarthjarta wasn't hiding anymore. It was inviting.

Within hours, Ydalir launched the Warborn fleet, three great Drakenships lined with runes and light-forged metal, shaped by both Earth and Zepharian hands.

On the bridge of the Hjartstorm, Erik Bloodaxe stood in ceremonial war-armor, the Eidrsigil strapped across his back. He carried no crown. He needed none.

Beside him, Astrid, now commander, seer, scientist, and
warrior, checked the Hjartablóð bracer one final time.

"You ready to challenge the future?" he asked.

"Only if it's brave enough to fight back," she answered.

Below, Earth watched. Across cities and nations, screens lit
up with the launch footage. Children cheered. Elders wept.
Others turned away. Some prayed to gods. Some prayed to
the stars. A few… prayed to the fire.

Before they breached the rift, Astrid recorded one final
transmission. Her voice was clear. Calm. And defiant.

"This is Astrid Jorgensen. We are not the chosen. We are not
pure. We are not perfect. But we are possible. And we will
not let the future be consumed. If we fall, let others rise.
If we burn, carry our spark. Because even the void fears
what we might become."

Then she ended the transmission. And Earth held its breath.

The ships vanished into the rift. The corridor swallowed
them without light. Without sound. Without promise.
But not without purpose. And on the other side… The future
waited. And the Svarthjarta prepared to kill it.

Chapter 12: The Return of the All-Thing

The ravens came at dawn. Two of them, silent, black as void, their wings stirring not the air but the threads of fate. They circled above Astrid as she stood atop the crystalline tower of Járnstóll, overlooking the blue curve of the Earth below. She didn't flinch when they landed on the rail beside her. Their eyes gleamed, not avian, but artificial. Ancient machines shaped like myth, cloaked in shadow and memory.

"Message carriers," Senrel said, appearing beside her. "Not ours."

Astrid didn't look away. She already knew.

"Odin's heralds."

The Zepharian cocked their head. "You speak of the Allfather as if he were real."

"He was real enough to Erik," she replied. "And real enough for whoever sent these."

One raven opened its beak. A scroll of light uncoiled from its throat, hovering in the air. The words burned in old Norse, edged with modern Zepharian glyphs.

"The clans call the All-Thing," Astrid read aloud. "To decide the fate of Midgard, the Flameborn, and the Pact."

Senrel's expression darkened, a rare flicker of concern. "They do not trust us."

"Good," Astrid said. "Trust is earned."

She turned to face the tower stair, bracer glowing.

"Prepare a skiff. We're going back to Earth."

"Where will you land?"

"Where all reckonings begin—Thingvellir."

The ravens took to the air, disappearing into a pale morning sky. Behind her, the Zepharian lights dimmed. And far below, the ancient ground of Iceland stirred, ready to host a gathering that had not occurred in a thousand years.

The Zepharian skiff descended like a falling star, silent and silver against the morning sky. The clouds parted as if pulled aside by ancient hands, revealing the jagged green scar of Thingvellir, cradled between mountains, where tectonic plates met and history had been hammered into legend.

Even from above, Astrid felt it. Not just the cool wind or the scent of ice and soil, but the weight of place. A thousand years of words had been spoken here: oaths, judgments, confessions, betrayals. The land remembered.

The skiff touched down on a field of black volcanic earth veined with glowing runes. A circle of stone stood at the clearing's edge, twenty slabs of basalt, each newly inscribed with clan sigils, both ancient and unfamiliar.

Already, others were arriving. Hovercrafts marked with Norse banners, red and black, blue and white, descended beside sleeker transports bearing the glyphs of the Flameborn enclaves. Warriors disembarked first, then chieftains and emissaries. Some wore furs. Others wore armored robes woven with light.

Astrid stepped onto the grass, flanked by Liv and Rurik. A hush fell over the gathering.

"That's her," someone murmured. "The Stormbearer. The Riftwalker."

"She walked beside Erik Bloodaxe," another said. "They say she still hears him speak."

A tall figure emerged from the far side of the circle, broad-shouldered, cloaked in storm-gray, his face lined by time but eyes sharp as ever.

Jorund Skarsgard, elder of the Eastern Fjordhold, and one of the few surviving members of Erik's original retinue.

"Astrid Jorgensen," he said, voice like thunder over still water. "Welcome home."

She clasped his forearm in the old warrior's grip.

"It's time, Jorund," she said. "The All-Thing must decide the future of Midgard."

He nodded slowly. "Then let us begin."

The stones of the Thingvellir Circle were older than any one clan, older even than the Viking Age itself. Some claimed they were laid by the first flamebearers, others, that they were carved by the gods in the days before time.

Today, they would bear witness again. Each representative took their place at a stone slab. No throne. No table. Only stone, sky, and blood-bound voices.

Astrid stood at the center. She did not wear armor. No weapon hung at her side. Her presence was her power, and the glowing Hjartablóð bracer on her forearm pulsed softly in the shadow of the morning sun.

Jorund raised a ceremonial staff of twisted iron and root.

"By right of the old ways, and by the flame of the new, I open this All-Thing. Who speaks first?"

A woman rose. Clad in a long black coat lined with steel-thread runes, she moved with the smooth control of a fighter and a diplomat. Her voice rang like tempered glass.

"I am Freydis Kolvardsdottir, of the northern skyholds. We were not asked to surrender our sons to Zepharian hands. We were told. And now our children return with power we cannot understand. I ask you, who rules Midgard now? The bloodline, or the machine?"

Murmurs rippled through the gathering. Some nodded. Others scowled.

Gunnar, leaning beside Astrid, muttered, "So it begins."

Astrid stepped forward.

"No one rules Midgard. Not the Zepharians. Not the Flamekind. And not the ghosts of our ancestors."

She scanned the circle.

"But someone must protect it. We all saw what came through the rift. The Svarthjarta wasn't legend. It was real. It still is."

A man to her left stood, bearded and robed in traditional black and green, Ulric Falnesson, chieftain of the western fjords.

"Then we should return to the old ways," he growled. "Steel and shield. Magic of the gods. Not this... alien mimicry."

"The gods didn't stop the Voidborn," Astrid said. "We did. With what we had. With what Erik was willing to risk everything to protect."

Silence returned. But the air was different now, charged. The All-Thing had begun. And it would not end quietly.

The sun climbed higher, casting sharp shadows between the stone seats. Though it was morning in Thingvellir, the temperature had dropped, as if the land itself sensed tension blooming like frost between ancient bloodlines. Jorund banged the ceremonial staff once more.

"Speak now, or be silent until war swallows your children."

A figure across the circle rose slowly. He wore no armor. No runes. Just a thick wool cloak and weathered hands, the skin marked by burns and calluses. His voice was low, patient, as if carved from the stone beneath his boots.

"I am Eirik Skelson. Farmer. Father. Once a raider. Now... just a man who still buries his dead when the frost lets go."

All eyes turned to him.

"You speak of old ways and alien fire like they're different monsters. But my son, Mikkel, he heard the call. Awakened. Went to the Forge. Came back... changed. Not monstrous. Not brainwashed. Better. More himself."
His voice cracked slightly.

"He stands taller. Fears less. Loves more. If the flame did that... then why would I fear it?"

A silence fell that was not discomfort, but consideration. Astrid exhaled slowly, the tension in her shoulders easing for the first time since the meeting began.

"Thank you," she said softly.

Freydis scoffed, breaking the silence.

"You'll trust the words of a dirt-hands farmer over the blood of kings?"

Eirik looked directly at her.

"It's not your blood that makes you noble. It's what you protect."

Even some of Freydis's allies didn't meet his gaze. The tide shifted, not fully, but perceptibly. And Astrid knew then: this wasn't just politics. It was identity at war with evolution. And the war had only just begun. The silence fractured with a single word.

"Holmgang."

Freydis's voice cut through the crisp air like an axe through birch.

Jorund turned slowly toward her. "You would invoke the rite of single combat?"

"She calls herself guardian of the flame," Freydis said, pointing at Astrid. "Let her prove her strength—not with speeches, but with steel."

Murmurs rose around the circle. The word hadn't been spoken in an All-Thing in centuries.

"This isn't about strength," Astrid replied, voice controlled. "It's about the survival of our world."

"And what survives if we let weak hands guide it?"

Astrid stepped forward, bracer glowing faintly. "You think I'm afraid of you?"

"No," Freydis said, smiling coldly. "I think you're afraid of what we've become, divided, uncertain, no longer bound by the gods we buried."

Jorund raised his staff. "Enough. The holmgang is an ancient right. If called in council, it must be answered."

"Then I accept," Astrid said without hesitation.

Gasps followed, some astonished, others admiring.

Gunnar leaned toward Liv, whispering, "She's insane."

"No," Liv replied, her gaze locked on Astrid. "She's honoring the old ways to protect the new."

Rurik stepped closer. "Let us fight for her."

"No," Astrid said, calm but final. "This is mine."

Jorund banged the staff. "Then let it be done."

He gestured to the side of the circle, where a smaller ring of stone and dirt had already been cleared. Two shields stood against a post. Two blades hung from iron hooks. No armor. No technology. Just the trial by flesh and will. The old gods stirred. And the people held their breath. The wind carried no sound as the two women stepped into the ring.

Around them, the All-Thing watched in grave silence. No jeering. No chants. Only respect for the rite, and for the blades about to be drawn in its name.

Astrid removed her bracer and laid it gently on a stone beside the ring. For the first time in months, she stood unarmored, unaugmented. Only the training from the Forge, at her side.

Freydis cracked her neck and chose the broadsword, its iron blade older than most of the gathering. She moved with the ease of someone born into battle, her posture perfect, her intent unmistakable: domination.

Astrid took the shorter seax blade and a round shield. She flexed her fingers, grounding herself.

Jorund's voice rang out:

"No blood beyond the ring. No death unless yielded. Trial ends when one cannot rise or yields in full."

He paused, eyes hard.

"Begin."

Freydis attacked immediately. Steel met steel with a shriek, sparks flying. Freydis's strength was overwhelming, each strike hammering down with the weight of a charging boar. Astrid blocked the first three, rolled to the side, and ducked under the fourth. She struck back, not to wound, but to test.

Freydis grinned. "You hesitate."

"No," Astrid replied. "I calculate."

Freydis swung again, faster this time. Astrid barely dodged, her shield absorbing the blow but splintering at the edge. She retreated, circling.

"Come now," Freydis taunted. "You preach unity, but you bleed like the rest of us."

"I'm not here to win your approval," Astrid said through gritted teeth. "Just your silence."

Freydis roared, lunging again, and Astrid saw it.

The pattern. A slight twist in the wrist, a pause in the inhale, Freydis's footwork gave her away. Astrid dropped low, slid under the next swing, and slammed the shield's edge into Freydis's knee. The warlady staggered. Gasps echoed. The holmgang had truly begun.

Freydis recovered quickly. Her knee buckled, but only for a heartbeat. She twisted mid-fall and swept her leg in a low arc, catching Astrid across the shins and knocking her sideways. Astrid landed hard on one shoulder, her seax skittering out of reach. Freydis loomed above her, sword raised.

"You talk of unity," she growled. "But you forget who we are. We're warriors. We conquer. Not bend the knee to alien whispers."

Astrid kicked upward with both legs, catching Freydis square in the ribs and sending her staggering backward. She rolled to her feet, snatching up the seax mid-motion.

"You think strength is the only truth," Astrid spat, circling. "But if that were enough, Erik wouldn't have had to wager everything on a future none of us fully understand."

Freydis's face twisted in a scowl. "Erik risked everything because he trusted ghosts."

Freydis's face twisted in a scowl. "Erik died because he trusted ghosts."

They clashed again, iron ringing against iron. This time, the crowd around the ring began to lean in, voices rising in quiet pulses of breath and tension. Astrid's strikes were precise, shaped by Zepharian cadence but driven by Norse instinct.

Freydis's blows were raw power, unrelenting, punishing.

Twice more, their blades locked. Sweat dripped from Astrid's brow. Her arms ached. Her ribs throbbed from a glancing blow. But her gaze never wavered.
And then—A mistake.

Freydis overcommitted on a downward slash. Her footing faltered for a fraction of a second. Astrid stepped inside her guard, slammed her shoulder into Freydis's sternum, and drove the seax forward, stopping just short of the other woman's neck. The blade hovered at the hollow of her throat.

"Yield," Astrid whispered. "You don't have to follow me. But you will not stop me."

The silence that followed was thicker than snow. Freydis's chest heaved. Her sword slipped from her fingers.

"I yield."

Freydis stepped back from the blade with slow, deliberate dignity. She did not look at Astrid again. Not out of shame, but concession. She had made her challenge. She had been answered. And though she still bore her doubts, she had honored the old law.

Astrid lowered the seax and tossed the cracked shield aside. Around them, murmurs stirred like wind through dry grass. Jorund raised his staff once more.

"The holmgang is decided. The challenge answered. Flamebearer Astrid remains in standing."

Freydis returned to her stone, silent, her warriors watching with unreadable eyes. Gunnar clapped once, sharp and deliberate. Others followed, hesitantly at first, then more confidently, until the ring echoed with slow, rhythmic applause. Not celebration. Recognition.

"Well fought," Liv said quietly as Astrid rejoined her. "You didn't kill her pride. Just tempered it."

"I don't want followers," Astrid replied, wiping sweat from her brow. "I want allies."

As the sun reached its zenith, the council reconvened. Freydis stood again, but this time, her voice held no heat.

"The old ways still live. But so must the new. I still question the Zepharians. But I no longer question her."

She nodded once toward Astrid.

"Let the council proceed."

One by one, the stones began to speak. Ulric Falnesson, once defiant, softened his tone. Eirik the farmer offered to host a Flamekind training enclave in the western fjords. Even the youngest emissaries, once silent, now leaned forward, hungry not just for resolution, but participation.

Senrel, standing at the periphery, whispered to Astrid.

"You've done what we could not."

"What's that?"

"Unified humans without war."

Astrid allowed herself a single breath of pride. But she knew the unity was still fragile. And far beyond the sky, the darkness was watching.

As the final votes were cast and oaths spoken, the air in Thingvellir changed. It was subtle at first, just a flicker of shadow across the sun, a sudden stillness in the birdsong overhead. But Astrid felt it in her bones. The ground was listening. And something above was whispering.

Jorund had just sealed the final pact—an agreement to establish the Flame Accord, a shared coalition of Norse, Flamekind, and Zepharian efforts, when a pulse of violet light shimmered across the sky. It wasn't natural. Not aurora. Not satellite. It was a warning.

Senrel stepped forward, speaking urgently in Zepharian, their voice broadcasting not through sound, but through thought, telepathic and immediate.

"We are receiving a distress signal from our outpost on the lunar rim. The words repeat: The Shadow Stirs. The Maw Opens."

Astrid's skin chilled. "Svarthjarta?"

Senrel nodded once.

"A precursor wave. Not a full incursion, but a sentient projection, a shadow-scout."

Freydis, still bruised but no longer hostile, clenched her fists.

"Then the time for talk is over."

"No," Astrid said. "It means the time for action has come."

Jorund turned to the gathered leaders.

"We have just built a pact. Now we must prove it means something."

The murmurs became pledges.

Rurik spoke. "I'll take the first strike team. Give me ten warriors and a Flamecraft shuttle."

Liv nodded. "Make it twelve. I'm coming too."

Gunnar thumped his chest. "You'll need thunder at your side."

Astrid stepped forward last, voice calm but commanding.

"The All-Thing is adjourned. But our war has just begun."

Above, the sky pulsed again. Not light. Not sound. But a single word in an ancient, alien voice:

"Soon."

The Flamecraft skiff rose once more from the soil of Thingvellir, bearing Astrid and her cadre into the stratosphere. This time, no one watched in silence.
Below, the gathered leaders of the All-Thing raised their fists in salute, Vikings, Awakened, elders, and emissaries all. Runes flared across banners. Ravens wheeled overhead. The pact had not been easy. It had been earned. And now it would be tested.

As the Earth fell away beneath the ship, Astrid moved to the command platform. Liv stood beside her, quiet and focused. Gunnar leaned against a bulkhead, helmet in his lap, humming an old funeral song. Rurik checked energy reserves on his staff-blade. Senrel joined them last, eyes turned toward the black horizon.

"The signal has gone quiet," they said. "But it was not false. Something is watching us."

"Good," Astrid replied. "Let it see what we're building."

Below her, the Earth glowed blue and white, beautiful, fragile, defiant.

"For a thousand years," she said, voice steady, "we lost our place in the stars. No more."

She turned to the group.

"You've trained. You've bled. You've doubted. But now we forge a legion. Not of conquest. Not of fear. But of flame."

Gunnar grinned. "We need a name."

Rurik shrugged. "We already have one."

Liv nodded. "The Warborn."

The word settled into place like a blade into its sheath.

"Then we ride as Warborn," Astrid said. "And we do not ride alone."

As Járnstóll appeared on the horizon, gleaming like a star-forge reborn, Astrid closed her eyes. She could almost hear Erik's voice.

"Keep the flame."

And in her chest, it burned. Not as a weapon. But as a promise.

Chapter 13: The Forge of the Stars

The carrier broke atmosphere in silence. Unlike the fiery roar of chemical rockets, the Zepharian-built transport lifted from Earth with a gentle pulse of gravitational manipulation. Below them, the mountains of Norway receded into a mist-draped sprawl. Above, the stars pulsed against the black.

Astrid sat near the forward viewport, her fingers flexing in her lap. The Hjartablóð bracer, now a permanent fixture on her arm, pulsed faintly with pale-blue runes, echoing her pulse. Around her sat twenty newly Awakened warriors, descendants of Erik Bloodaxe, touched by the same resonance that had called to her.

"You all feel it," she said aloud. "Like your body doesn't fit quite right anymore."

Murmurs of agreement filled the cabin. One man, broad and tattooed with old Norse knots, nodded.

"My senses feel too big. I can hear the heartbeats of people two rows back."

"Mine too," a younger woman whispered. "And... I dream in languages I don't know."

Astrid turned toward the center aisle, where a tall, silver-robed Zepharian stood with folded hands. Their name was Senrel, and their face held no expression, but their luminous eyes glinted like starlight on steel.

"These sensations are normal," Senrel intoned. "You are not changing. You are returning to what your blood remembers."

The cabin fell into hushed awe as they pierced the clouds and entered low orbit. Ahead of them, emerging from shadow, the training station revealed itself, Járnstóll.

Forged of crystal, alloy, and shaped gravity, it resembled a forge hammer drifting through the stars. Vast, jagged, ringed with pylons of radiant silver, it shimmered with Zepharian design, but at its core, embedded in its hull, was the unmistakable mark of Norse influence: a dragon-head prow welded into place. A blend of old and new. A crucible for what the Awakened might become.

"Welcome," Senrel said, "to the Forge of the Stars."

The docking arms of Járnstóll unfolded like limbs of a mechanical beast, embracing the incoming carrier with uncanny precision. Magnetic seals clicked into place with a hiss of pressurized air. The moment the gravity field adjusted, the cabin lights dimmed to violet, signaling descent.

Astrid was the first to rise. Her boots hit the deck with a resonant thud that echoed like a heartbeat across the chamber. One by one, the Awakened followed, some hesitantly, others with the eager posture of warriors entering a long-hoped-for battlefield.

The air on Járnstóll was different. Not just colder but it tasted of ozone and old things. Runes inlaid in the walls pulsed with soft energy, responding to the presence of their human guests. The entire structure felt alive, not merely mechanical, but aware, like a ship with memory.

They passed through a corridor lit by arcing bands of colorless light, their steps muffled by some unseen field. As they approached the inner sanctum, Senrel raised a hand.

"Here is where we begin."

A vast chamber opened before them. Circular. Tiered like a coliseum. In the center, a dais rose from the floor, its surface composed of shifting crystal and stone. The walls bore etched scenes, not Zepharian, but Norse: longships crossing alien oceans, wolves and ravens spiraling through stars, and a bearded man wielding an axe of starlight—Erik.

Astrid's breath caught. The likeness was unmistakable.

"You honor him," she said.

Senrel inclined their head.

"We honor what he became. As we will now shape what *you* may become."

A hum began to vibrate through the floor. The dais cracked open, revealing six portals, each glowing with different elemental light: fire, ice, void, storm, metal, and thought.

"These are the Ættar Trials," Senrel announced. "Each of you must pass through. Alone. You do not choose the element. It chooses you."

Someone swallowed hard behind Astrid. Another whispered a prayer to Odin. She stepped forward, expression firm.

"Then let it choose."

And the portal of stormlight flared in response. The portal consumed her in an instant. No time to think, no turning back. The light seared across her vision like a blade drawn through glass, and then, she fell. Wind screamed past her ears, raw and ancient. Thunder cracked above like the laughter of forgotten gods. She landed hard on a stone outcropping jutting from the side of a jagged cliff, suspended over an endless sea of churning black water.

Above, the sky boiled. Clouds twisted in impossible shapes, spitting lightning that danced like angry spirits. The scent of ozone and salt filled her nostrils, and her skin prickled with static.

"Where…?" she breathed.

Then, a voice, not external, but vibrating through her bones.

"You are within yourself."

The storm did not abate. It surged, answering her fear with fury. A shape approached along the cliff, massive, limping, dragging a broken sword across the stone. A figure cloaked in tattered armor, its eyes glowing like moons in shadow. It was Erik. But not as he had been.

This version was fractured, flickering between his living form and a charred husk. His voice echoed with both warmth and pain.

"The storm is not your enemy," he said. "It is your inheritance."

"What does that mean?" she demanded.

"You fear your strength. You bury your fury. But storm is not chaos. It is *focus.* Channeled rage. Righteous power."

He raised his sword, and pointed it at her.

"Prove that you are worthy of it."

Then the world exploded into wind and war. A cyclone descended, and Astrid stood at the edge, her bracer glowing with blue fire.

"I won't fight you," she shouted.

"You already are."

Lightning struck. And Astrid screamed, not in pain, but in release, as she stepped into the heart of the storm. The storm should have torn her apart. Winds shrieked like dying gods. Bolts of raw lightning split the cliffside, hurling shards of stone into the maelstrom. Yet Astrid stood firm, bracer raised, her boots grinding against the slick rock.

Every instinct screamed to run. To protect herself. To survive. But something deeper pulsed in her blood, a rhythm, steady and undeniable, like the old war drums of her ancestors. And beneath it, a question that burned hotter than the lightning: Who are you without fear?

A vortex surged toward her, and Erik's phantom voice roared through the wind:

"If you do not claim the storm, it will claim you!"

The wind slammed into her chest like a hammer, lifting her off her feet. For a moment, she tumbled through sky, flailing—and then something shifted. She remembered. She remembered her mother's trembling hands when she first told her of the dreams. She remembered standing alone in a lecture hall, defending a theory no one believed. She remembered kneeling beside Erik's broken body, watching him march into the rift, and being too late to follow.
The storm wasn't testing her. It was her.

She stopped falling. And started flying. Wings of blue-white energy surged from her shoulders. Not literal, but forged of will and defiance. Her descent slowed. She turned midair and rose, eyes alight with the storm's fury. When she landed, it was in the center of the maelstrom. Erik's figure faded into mist. The wind died. And silence reigned.

Then, above her, a new rune formed in the sky, Eirvindr, the ancient word for storm-bearer. The bracer burned the symbol into her skin. She opened her eyes in the chamber of Járnstóll. Senrel stood waiting.

"You have passed," they said.

"No," Astrid replied softly. "I've only begun."

As Astrid stepped down from the glowing platform, her eyes still haloed with stormlight, the next Awakened was already being chosen. The portal of fire ignited in a column of crimson light.

"Gunnar Thorssen," Senrel intoned. "The forge calls you."

Gunnar stepped forward with a swagger barely hiding his nerves. His red beard bristled with static. He cast a glance at Astrid, a half-grin twitching at the corner of his mouth.

"Hope the storm didn't rattle you too much," he said. "I'm more of a wildfire man myself."

Then he vanished into flame. The air shimmered with residual heat, and moments later, the ice portal bloomed. From its center stepped a woman barely twenty, Liv Isedottir, one of the youngest Awakened. She moved with caution, her dark braids tightly bound, her expression stoic. She did not speak before entering. Her trial, like Gunnar's, was hers alone.

From across the chamber, Astrid watched the glow of the portals shift, blue flame dancing beside a vortex of frozen mist. She could almost hear the echoes of their experiences, though no sound escaped the elemental trials.

Senrel turned to her.

"They will not all return as you have."

"What happens if they fail?"

"They are not destroyed. But their path is sealed. Without harmony between body, will, and legacy, they cannot ascend."

Astrid's gaze drifted toward the remaining portals: void, metal, thought. More would step forward. Some would rise. Others would break. But together, they were forging something new. Not merely warriors. Not merely descendants.

"We're building a people," Astrid whispered. "Not an army."

"That," Senrel replied, "is what makes you dangerous."

The chamber of the Ættar Trials dimmed as the final portal closed. Of the twenty Awakened brought to Járnstóll, sixteen had passed. Two had emerged wounded, spiritually or otherwise. Two more had not returned. They were not dead. But neither were they the same. Senrel called them "marked." Their trials incomplete. Their potential, dormant.

But for the sixteen who passed, the next phase began. The Gravedeck was nothing like the crystalline halls of the Forge's central spire. It was cold steel and jagged edges designed not for elegance but pressure. Gravity fluctuated every few minutes, forcing constant adaptation. One moment light as mist, the next heavy as stone. Astrid landed hard after a missed vault, her breath knocked from her lungs.

"Again!" barked the drillmaster, a towering Warborn named Skorr One-Eye, whose flesh was half rune-ink and half Zepharian alloy. "You fall like birds. I want to see *wolves!*"

Beside her, Gunnar landed in a crouch, grinning.

"Bet I beat you to the top this time."

"I don't need to beat you," Astrid muttered. "Just need to outlast you."

Their banter ended when Liv charged past both, silent as a glacier, vaulting through the gravity surge with precise control. Her bracer glinted frost. Skorr roared with approval.

"That's what I want! Not just bloodline, but balance! You want to wear the runes? You earn them."

Behind them, the two "marked" Awakened, Kjell and Siv, watched from the shadows. They did not speak. They did not train. But their eyes were cold with envy.

Later, as the training cycle ended and the gravity returned to normal, Astrid sat with Liv beneath a crystal arch.

"You're quiet," she said.

"Ice doesn't boast," Liv replied, "it breaks things when needed."

Astrid smiled faintly. The forge was doing its work. But pressure did not only shape. It also cracked. The Forge never slept. It drifted above the Earth in eternal rotation, bathed in starlight and shadow. Within its depths, training continued. Weapons formed. Minds sharpened. But beneath the surface, something darker began to stir, doubt.

At the end of the third cycle, the Awakened gathered in the Yngrdome, a common area carved of reinforced crystal and alloy, where food and fire were shared. The hearth, shaped like a dragon's maw, burned without fuel, its flame conjured by Zepharian technology, but blue as glacial ice.

Gunnar leaned against the edge of a pillar, arms folded.

"You ever wonder," he said, "why they're giving us all this?"

Astrid, sipping from a steaming flask of brewed mossleaf, glanced sideways. "Giving?"

"Training. Weapons. Orbiting palaces. All of it. They say they don't want anything, but that's never true. Not in war. Not in blood."

From across the room, Kjell nodded. He hadn't spoken in days, but his eyes followed Gunnar like iron to lodestone.

"He's right," Kjell finally said. "The Zepharians want something. They're shaping us. Like we're a tool."

"Or a weapon," Liv added, stepping into the circle. Her tone was calm, but her hand hovered close to the frost-hilted blade on her hip.

Astrid stood slowly, setting the flask aside.

"They're not shaping us. They're testing us. To see what we become when given the chance."

"And if they don't like what we become?" Gunnar asked.

"Do they have another rift to toss us into?"

The room fell quiet. Senrel, who had arrived unnoticed, stepped into the firelight. Their robes shimmered with auroral hues.

"Doubt is part of becoming," they said. "So is resistance. But know this, your strength lies not in your bloodline, nor your training. It lies in the choices you make when the storm comes."

Kjell's lip curled. Gunnar looked away. Astrid held her ground. And the fire between them burned brighter than before.

The fourth cycle began like any other, until it didn't. During the zero-gravity weapons trial, Kjell was partnered with Rurik Halvardson, a soft-spoken flame-channeler who had scored top marks in every element-focused discipline. The two had never spoken beyond nods. They were never meant to clash. But then, Kjell lost control.

Rurik's blade struck high, not hard enough to injure, but precise. A reminder that skill mattered more than strength.

"Tighter grip," Rurik said calmly. "Your stance leaves you open."

Kjell snarled.

"I don't need advice from someone who didn't even pass the Trial of Metal."

Rurik stepped back, surprised. "It's not a competition, brother."

But Kjell was already moving. His bracer surged with unstable voidlight, twisting, irregular. Not sanctioned energy. A forbidden resonance. He struck. Rurik barely raised a defense. The impact sent him crashing into the Gravedeck wall, where his armor sparked and hissed. Sirens screamed.

Astrid arrived seconds later, leaping from the upper tier of the arena. Liv followed, blade drawn.

"Stand down, Kjell!" Astrid shouted, lightning crackling from her bracer.

But he didn't stop. The voidlight pulsed again and this time, it struck the ceiling. Metal warped. The gravity field destabilized. Everything lurched.

Suddenly, Astrid and Liv were pinned against the deck, their weight multiplied tenfold. Senrel entered the chamber, arms raised, eyes flaring white.

"ENOUGH."

With a single gesture, the voidlight dispersed. The pressure dropped. The room returned to balance. Rurik groaned from the far wall, conscious but dazed. Kjell stood frozen, chest heaving, his hands still flickering with remnant power.

"He provoked me," he muttered.

"You almost killed him," Astrid snapped. "And half of us with him."

"You think you're the only one who hears the storm?" Kjell growled. "You think you're the only one worthy?"

He turned away, seething. Senrel stepped forward, gaze unreadable.

"You are no longer permitted to train."

Kjell did not protest. He simply walked into the shadows. And was gone. The Gravedeck remained closed for an entire cycle. No drills. No gravity shifts. No elemental flows. Silence.

The injury to Rurik had shaken more than bones. It cracked the illusion that power alone would carry them forward. The Awakened had come to the Forge believing themselves chosen heirs to a legacy both divine and technological. Now, some questioned if they deserved it at all.

In the central gallery, Astrid stood before the etched mural of Erik Bloodaxe, half man, half flame, holding back the void. She stared into his eyes, carved in silver-stone.

"We're not ready," she said aloud.

Liv approached behind her. "You are. Some of us are. But others…"

"They're fractured. Lost. We pulled power from the stars without preparing hearts to carry it."

Liv nodded solemnly. "Kjell's not the only one who's been dreaming strange things. I see black skies when I sleep. Stars being swallowed."

"The Svarthjarta," Astrid whispered.

Just then, Senrel entered. "Good. You are gathered."

Others began arriving, Gunnar, bruised and brooding; Rurik, his arm bandaged but his eyes focused; even a few of the quieter Awakened, newly uncertain.

"You have faced the elements," Senrel said. "You have trained in motion and thought. But now, a more difficult challenge awaits."

A holographic field ignited at the room's center, displaying a simulation of a rift incursion, Voidborn entities breaching atmosphere, attacking a human outpost near the old Arctic Circle.

"You will face this trial not alone, but as a unit. Strength will not save you. Not if you fight like wolves."

"So what will?" Gunnar asked.

Senrel turned to Astrid.

"Flame," she said, stepping forward. "And the will to burn together."

The trial began at dawn. The simulation began with fire. The Zepharian chamber dissolved, replaced by cold air, cragged cliffs, and the dim flicker of a collapsing outpost nestled in the Arctic ruins. The Awakened materialized in full armor, rune-infused exo-shells tailored to their elemental affinities. Their weapons pulsed with dormant power, now unlocked by training and will.

"Voidborn incoming," Astrid said, reading the holographic scan flickering across her helm. "Three fronts. Fast approach. Watch for phase flicker."

Rurik moved to the flank, bracing his heat-spear in one arm and planting a power stake into the ground with the other.

"Shield line set."

Gunnar unslung his pulse-hammer and grinned. "Let's make 'em regret every breath they ever stole."

Liv said nothing, slipping into the snow-shadow with icy precision. Her blade gleamed with frost-rune light. They didn't speak again. Because the Voidborn arrived.

Shifting masses of shadow and sound, forms that vibrated with forgotten hunger. They lunged, striking with limbs of smoke and talons. The Awakened responded not with panic, but with coordination.

Gunnar broke the line with a forward slam, creating a shockwave. Rurik and Astrid followed with alternating blasts of heat and lightning, combining in a spiral of converging destruction. Liv struck from the rear, cutting through weak points in their armor like a ghost made of vengeance. And when the second wave emerged from the cliff's edge, the team turned in a perfect pivot, reacting not from command but intuition. The battle lasted eleven minutes. They won in eight.

When the simulation dropped, silence reigned. Senrel stood at the chamber's edge, arms folded. Slowly, they nodded.

"You are not yet a legion. But you are becoming one."

Astrid turned to her companions—bloodied, bruised, breathing hard. And smiled.

"Let's see what else we can become."

Above them, the Forge of the Stars pulsed with light. The first flame had been lit. The forge went silent. The warriors stood ready. And the stars, long indifferent, now watched.

Chapter 14: The Breach

The lunar surface had not known war for millennia.
But now, it shuddered. Járnstóll's outer satellites blinked crimson as the alert pulsed through the station. A rift, a true rift, had begun to open near the Tycho Crater, its coordinates twisting between physical dimensions and voidspace echoes. No natural phenomenon could mimic the energy signature. This was Svarthjarta-born.

Astrid stood before the Forge's command spire, surrounded by her hand-picked team. Liv, Gunnar, Rurik, and six other Awakened, all clad in advanced rune-armor newly forged for zero-atmosphere combat. Each bore a Flameborn core linked to the Hjartablóð matrix.

"This isn't a simulation," Astrid said, voice calm but heavy. "We don't get to fail and try again."

Rurik tightened the bindings on his forearm. "Do we have confirmation on what's coming through?"

Senrel's image flickered into view, projected from the Zepharian archive.

"No direct visual. But the rift echoes… they match what Erik faced at Valhalheim. This is not a probe. It is a feeler. A test. The Svarthjarta seeks to know your defenses."

"Then we answer in full," Liv said, eyes cold as ice.

A deep hum filled the air as the Warborn's assault ship, the Naglfar's Flame, ignited its core. Unlike the older Drakenskip models, this vessel had no heritage but the present. It was flame and will made metal.

Astrid gripped the command rail.

"Warborn. This is our threshold. We don't hold the line. We are the line."

And with that, the ship launched into the void.

The Naglfar's Flame exited sublight in a silent ripple of distortion, emerging just beyond the jagged rim of the Tycho Crater. The moon hung below them, a sea of ash and stone pockmarked by eons of impact. Above, the stars were frozen witnesses. But directly ahead was distortion.

The rift hadn't fully opened, but it pulsed like a wound in reality. A swirling knot of obsidian and amethyst, bending light inward, as if the void was tasting the world before devouring it. Around it, space itself shimmered like a mirage. Fragments of unknown matter floated outward in slow spirals.

Gunnar leaned forward at the viewport.

"That's not natural."

"No," Liv said. "That's hunger given shape."

Sensors flickered across the ship's interface. Rurik swept his hand over a rune-display, casting an infrared grid across the anomaly.

"No heat signature. No gravity. But the voidmatter is reacting to our presence."

"How long before it stabilizes into a full gate?" Astrid asked. Senrel's voice came over comms, distant and filtered through static.

"Less than an hour. Once the breach stabilizes, it will begin pulling. Not just matter. Thought. Soul. You must disrupt it before then."

"Then we don't wait," Astrid said. "Warborn, deploy."

The ship's hull unfolded in a complex ballet of moving panels, revealing launch platforms lined with shimmering drop spears, Zepharian tech redesigned with Norse aggression. Each Warborn stood within their own, weapons humming, eyes set on the unnatural tide below.

"Brace for lunar descent," the AI intoned.

Astrid clenched her fists.

"For Midgard. For flame."

And with a hiss of light and silence, they fell to war.

The drop spears struck the lunar surface like divine bolts, embedding themselves in the regolith around the breach site. Dust plumed upward in slow, silent spirals, each granule suspended longer than it should be, as if the laws of physics were second-guessing themselves this close to the rift.

Astrid emerged first, her boots crunching softly in the moon's brittle dust. Her armor adjusted to the low gravity with subtle shifts in balance and pressure, powered by the Hjartablóð matrix now humming like a distant heartbeat. She turned slowly.

The rift loomed ahead like a bruise in the stars. It hadn't grown, but it had deepened. Its center pulsed with a dark rhythm, slower now, as though it was listening. Then came the sound.

A vibration, not through the air, for there was none, but through the bones. A low thrum of presence, ancient and mournful. The kind of sound you feel behind the eyes. The kind that makes you forget your own name.

"Void-speech," Rurik said, stepping beside her, spear ready.

"It's not words. It's invitation."

"To what?" Gunnar growled. "Dinner?"

Liv unslung her twin blades, now radiating a shimmer of frost.

"It's calling to something."

As if on cue, the ground beneath them shifted. What they had mistaken for boulders began to move, unfolding in jerking, insectile spasms. Shapes with too many joints. Limbs of glassy blackness. Heads that bore no eyes, only mouths. Dozens of them. One rose fully, standing twice the height of a man, its chest a hollow void of writhing mist.

"Voidborn," Astrid whispered.

The lead creature opened its jaw, not to roar, but to echo, a perfect mimicry of Erik's voice.

"You are too late."

Astrid's eyes flared.

"No. We're right on time."

And she charged.

The moment Astrid's boots left the ground, time fractured. She struck the lead Voidborn mid-lunge, her lightning-forged axe cleaving through its mist-cloaked arm. The limb disintegrated into vapor, not blood, not bone, but something that remembered both. The creature screamed, though the sound came not from its mouth, but from the minds of the Warborn.

"Protect the breach perimeter!" Astrid shouted across the comms. "No matter what comes through!"

The lunar field erupted into motion. Gunnar launched into the fray like a comet, his hammer blazing with solar heat. He collided with two Voidborn, scattering them across the regolith. Each strike cracked the airless silence with ripples of kinetic force that left long, glowing scars in the lunar dust.

"You want to whisper in my head?" he growled, crushing another foe. "Let's see how you scream!"

To the north, Liv became a blur of motion, her frostblades slicing through shadows like wind through silk. She fought without rage, without sound, only precision. Where her blades struck, ice bloomed, freezing the Voidborn from within, shattering their hollow cores like crystal.

Rurik held the center line, his rune-staff pulsing with wave after wave of searing energy. He spun in tight arcs, creating barriers of heat and resonance that deflected the acidic tendrils launched by a new class of Voidborn, smaller, faster, almost reptilian in motion.

"They're adapting," Rurik warned. "Every strike teaches them something!"

"Then we stop teaching," Astrid snapped. "And start ending."

One Voidborn lunged toward her blind side, but a spear of hardlight impaled it mid-air. Behind her, the youngest Warborn, Elya Jornsdottir, nodded nervously, her bracer smoking from the shot.

"I've got your six, Commander."

"Good," Astrid replied, stepping over a twitching body. "Let's make sure we keep it."

Above them, the rift pulsed again, brighter now. It was opening further. The first wave had been the stormfront. The real breach was still coming.

The rift changed. Where once it shimmered like a warped mirror, it now beat like a heart, every throb sending a pulse of black energy across the lunar surface. The Warborn could feel it in their chests, in their thoughts, pulling not just at their bodies, but at their convictions.

Astrid stumbled for half a step, the world tilting sideways. In that instant, she wasn't on the moon. She was on Earth. A burning city. Screaming faces. The charred ruins of Járnstóll collapsing above a broken planet.

"Astrid!" Liv's voice sliced through the illusion.

Astrid blinked, stumbled back into reality just as a Voidborn's claw swiped across her shield. Sparks flared. Her armor held.

"It's the rift," she gasped. "It's pushing visions. Doubt. Fear."

"Then we give it something to fear back," Gunnar growled, lifting a cratered boulder and hurling it through a cluster of lesser Voidborn.

Behind them, Rurik knelt at the center of a glowing hexagraph. He was constructing a containment lattice, a Zepharian failsafe, forbidden to humans until now.

"Give me sixty seconds," he called. "But when I activate it, we'll all be locked in until it's done."

"That's fine," Astrid said, cutting down another shrieking shadow. "We weren't planning on running anyway."

More creatures emerged from the rift, some fused together, forming grotesque amalgamations of limbs and mouths. They moved faster, more coordinated.

"They're learning from us," Liv warned. "Mirroring tactics."
"Then we break the mirror," Astrid snarled.

She raised her weapon, now pulsing not just with lightning, but with memory. Erik's voice echoed inside her again, not as a ghost, but as resolve:

"The void will take your fear. Give it fire instead."

Astrid surged forward, cutting down the front line. Time was running out. The lattice had to hold. Or nothing would.

Rurik's voice cut across the comms, resolute and low:

"Lattice activating... now."

A shockwave of light erupted from the hexagraph embedded in the lunar crust. Six pillars of fire-forged runes spiraled into the sky, forming a dome of translucent gold. Where the light passed, Voidborn recoiled, some shrieking, others convulsing before disintegrating into wisps of voidmist. But many survived. And those that did became faster. Smarter.

The containment field stabilized with a thunderous hum. Inside it, the battle would now finish, one way or another.

Gunnar stumbled as the gravity shifted. "We just boxed ourselves in with nightmares."

"Correction," Rurik said, rising from the center. "We boxed the nightmares in with us."

The battlefield shrank. Every crater became a kill zone. Every exposed angle a vulnerability. The Voidborn adapted again, now leaping over defensive lines, weaving between attacks, striking in coordinated waves.

Elya fell, her shoulder punctured by a claw. Astrid dragged her behind a boulder, firing a bolt of pure kinetic force from her bracer, reducing the assailant to vapor.

"Status!" Astrid barked. "Who's down?"

"Gunnar's shield's compromised," Liv reported. "My right blade's fractured. Rurik's draining power fast."

"Fallback to the inner ring. Form the Valknut."

The Warborn responded instantly, arranging themselves into a tri-point phalanx, a strategy first tested in simulations, never in live battle. From above, the rift pulsed again.
And something stepped through.

It wasn't like the others. It stood tall, humanoid in shape, armored in flickering void-metal that shimmered like glass under starlight. Its face bore no features, only the outline of where a face should be. And it spoke.

"Children of fire. You burn too brightly."

Astrid felt a chill ripple through her spine. The Svarthjarta had sent a Herald.

The Herald moved like shadow wrapped in armor, each step displacing not dust, but light. Its hands were long and clawed, yet elegant, like a twisted mirror of the Zepharians.

The runes on Astrid's armor dimmed as it approached. It was not just a creature. It was a voice. A message.

"You are not ready," it said in a voice that echoed from within every Warborn's mind. "You wear flame like children wear crowns."

Astrid stepped forward, tightening her grip on her axe.

"We've bled for this flame. Burned for it."

"And so you shall. The void does not hate. It simply corrects."

The Herald moved with impossible speed, one moment twenty meters away, the next, swinging a blade of starless metal toward Astrid's throat. She blocked by instinct, her axe screaming under the pressure. Sparks scattered like meteor trails.

Liv flanked right, blades flashing, but the Herald turned without turning, catching one strike mid-air and twisting the frost-steel until it cracked.

"You copy power," it said. "You do not understand it."

Rurik launched a blast of radiant heat toward the Herald's back. The creature vanished, blinked, and reappeared behind him, untouched.

Gunnar roared and slammed his hammer into the lunar ground, sending up a wall of debris, but the Herald sliced through it with a gesture, untouched.

"We'll take it together," Astrid barked. "Focus!"

The Warborn converged, moving as one. Liv swept low. Gunnar struck high. Rurik lit the dome with solar arcs. Astrid came down center, driving her blade into the Herald's chest. For a moment, just one, its armor cracked. Darkness spilled from the wound. Not blood. Not matter. A memory. A scream. A world dying. The Herald hissed and struck outward, sending all four warriors flying.

It did not pursue. It simply stood.

"You are fire," it said, voice dimming. "But we are night. And night is long."

Then, in a blink of voidlight, it vanished. The rift pulsed once more. And began to close.

The rift sealed with a soundless thrum, like a breath being exhaled by the moon itself. The warped energy that had crackled across the crater faded, leaving behind only scorched stone, shattered Voidborn remains, and silence.

The containment lattice flickered, then collapsed in a slow shimmer, returning gravity and light to their natural balance. Astrid staggered to her feet, coughing dust from her lungs. Her axe was chipped. Her armor was cracked along the left pauldron. Her hands still trembled, not from fatigue, but from what she had seen in the Herald's eyes. A dying world. A sun snuffed out like a candle. The last thought of a child as it vanished into darkness.

Liv leaned against a broken ridge, one of her frostblades bent nearly in half. Blood smeared her cheek. She didn't speak.

Rurik was on his knees, arms wrapped around his core brace. The lattice draw had drained him. His glow was dim. Gunnar limped over, dragging his hammer behind him like a wounded limb.

"Well. That sucked."

Astrid managed a small, grim smile. "We're alive."

"Barely," Liv muttered. "That thing wasn't just faster. It knew us. It studied us in real-time."

"It mocked us," Rurik added. "Like we were schoolchildren with torches."

Astrid looked around at the field. Elya was receiving aid from two Warborn medics. Three others sat in a circle, silent, armor scorched.

"We won," she said.

"Did we?" Gunnar asked. "Or did it just... test us?"

No one answered. A flicker of movement appeared in the sky, three Zepharian ships, arriving in staggered formation. They landed in silence, doors hissing open. Senrel stepped into the dust.

"The rift has closed," they said. "But it will not be the last. You must all understand that now."

Astrid stood taller, though the weight in her chest remained.

"We understand."

"Then prepare," Senrel said. "Because next time, the Herald won't be alone."

The Zepharian medical teams moved quickly, administering regenerative nanosealant to the wounded, lifting damaged suits into support shells. But Astrid stood apart from it all, eyes locked on Senrel as the ambassador studied the crater left behind by the closed rift.

"You knew," she said.

Senrel didn't turn. "We suspected."

"You knew." Her voice rose. "That the Svarthjarta weren't just myths. That they had Heralds. That they were watching. Why didn't you warn us?"

Senrel finally turned, expression unreadable.

"Because knowledge without readiness is despair. Erik understands that. It's why he chose to leave and not return until the flame had taken root."

"And you just watched?" Astrid said, stepping closer.

"Letting Earth forget while you waited for us to earn a truth you were too afraid to share?"

"We were not afraid. We were... uncertain," Senrel replied.

"The last time we confronted the Svarthjarta directly, entire systems fell into silence. Entire species vanished. What came through the rift today was only a whisper of their reach."
"Then why help us at all?"

Senrel's voice lowered. "Because you're different. Humans fight through fear. You do not obey entropy, you defy it. That defiance may be the only thing the void cannot consume."

Astrid looked away, jaw clenched.

"You should've trusted us."

"We are trusting you now. You fought the Herald and survived. That is more than any other world has done."

A silence passed. Then Astrid said:

"I want access to your archives. Everything on the Svarthjarta. I'm done playing blind."

Senrel tilted their head. "Access will be granted. But know this, Astrid Jorgensen: the truth may break more than it builds."

"So will the void," she said. "And we're still standing."

The moon's surface was quiet now. Too quiet. The rift was sealed. The Herald gone. The wounded tended. Yet every Warborn knew: this had not been a victory. It had been a warning.

Inside the Naglfar's Flame, the surviving squad gathered in the central chamber. Armor scorched. Spirits drained. But eyes? Still burning. Astrid stood at the head of the chamber, her axe leaning against the bulkhead, her hands braced on the edge of the holotable where a projection of the Svarthjarta Herald still flickered in warped fragments.

"This is what waits," she said. "This is what we were Awakened to stop."

No one interrupted.

Gunnar crossed his arms. "We nearly died today."

"Yes," Astrid said. "And we will again. But we didn't break. We didn't run. We didn't turn against each other. That's the difference. That's what makes us *Warborn*."

Liv nodded. "We can train for speed. For power. But nothing trains you for truth."

"So we train harder," Rurik said. "And we find the others. Not just more Awakened, but more who still believe in a world worth saving."

Elya raised her head from a medbay seat. "What if there aren't enough of us?"

Astrid looked at her.

"Then we'll make enough flame to light the stars."

A quiet fell over the ship. Then, one by one, each of them placed their bracer over the holotable. The runes glowed in synchronized gold. A pact renewed. Not by blood. By choice. By fire. And somewhere in the cold silence between worlds... The Svarthjarta stirred. But so did the light.

Chapter 15: Embers of Unity

The rain came sideways—slashing, sleeting, metallic. In the forests outside Trondheim, the world once known for pine trees and quiet winters now bore the shape of a battlefield. Lightning streaked across the sky, not natural but flaring with Zepharian color, tinged violet-blue. It reflected off smoldering wrecks and shattered bunkers. Smoke coiled like wounded serpents.

Astrid Jorgensen crouched low behind a scorched Drakenskip husk, her armor cracked and sparking, her pulse hammering. They were losing ground.

"East flank's gone," Liv's voice crackled through the comm. "Civilians caught in the retreat path. Erik's force is pinched in the gorge."

"Pull the refugees toward Ridge 3," Astrid replied. "We'll hold this corridor as long as we can."

She peered over the rise. In the distance, one of the Svarthjarta feeder-creatures crawled across the terrain like a spider made of thoughts and bone. Its limbs dug through soil not for traction, but for memories. Where it passed, the terrain changed. Buildings forgot their shape. Roads bent wrong.

"How the hell are they already on the surface?" Elya's voice snapped. "I thought the breach was still holding."

"They didn't come through it," Astrid said grimly. "They grew here."

Liv swore softly. "Grew?"

"They've seeded the planet. They've been waiting."

She rose to her feet and ignited the runes on her axe.

"Then we rip out the roots."

"Contact Erik's command," Astrid barked. "Tell him I'm pushing west with a fallback perimeter."

She vaulted over the wreckage, sprinting toward the next ridge with Liv and two Flameborn warriors at her side. Her boots kicked through shattered stone and fragments of memory—the kind left behind when Voidborn had scraped at reality.

Over comms, Elya's voice came back: "No signal from Erik. Járnstóll link is jammed. He might already be surrounded." Astrid gritted her teeth. "Then we improvise."

To the south, columns of smoke rose above the treeline. Not black like fuel fire. Blue-white. Flameborn defensive lines had lit their skybeacons. That meant one thing: civilian unrest. Again.

In a burned-out village on the northern coast, a crowd of refugees had turned on their Flameborn protectors. Armed with salvaged rifles and old military-grade EMP weapons, they formed a ring around a Valkari squad attempting to usher evacuees into Zepharian dropcraft.

"Step back!" a Valkari officer shouted, blood on her cheek. "We're trying to move you to safety!"

A grizzled militia leader, with scars on his neck, and a patch over one eye, stepped forward.

"You're not human. You're what brought them here. You and your damn runes."

"You'd rather die?" she asked, stunned.

"I'd rather die free."

The crowd surged.

Astrid and Liv arrived just as the crowd broke through the Valkari line. Liv fired a warning shot into the air, runed frost detonating like a flare.

"That's enough!" Astrid shouted, voice amplified by her suit.

"They're here to help you."

One man raised a rifle. Liv's blade was at his throat in less than a second.

"Try it," she hissed. "See how far your fear carries you."

The man dropped the weapon. Astrid faced the crowd.

"We can't win divided. You hate us because we changed. But you will not survive what's coming unless we change together."

Behind her, the sky shimmered. A Svarthjarta specter stepped through the veil. And everyone forgot what they were arguing about.

The Voidborn specter towered over the crowd, twelve feet tall, cloaked in shadows that writhed like a living cloak. Its head bore no face, only a shifting mask of reflected memories. Someone screamed. Then it attacked.

With a thought, it shredded part of the village square. A sphere of reality simply collapsed, buildings and trees swallowed in an instant. The crowd panicked, scattering. Children cried. Rifles fired, but the bullets twisted in midair and turned to dust.

Astrid lunged. Her axe ignited with Zepharian-core light, runes flashing like stars under skin. She struck at the beast's side, cleaving into the shifting veil. The creature staggered, not hurt, but surprised. Few things hurt them. Even fewer dared.

Liv joined the fray, flanking it with twin daggers of frosted plasma. She sliced through its lower limbs, causing it to falter. The thing let out a soundless howl that was felt more in the bones than in the ears.

"Hit it with memory anchors!" Astrid shouted. "Remind it we're real."

Flameborn adepts moved in, projecting rune-seals into the air, personal totems, echoes of family, ancestral chants encoded in light. As they formed around the beast, it shrieked and began to unravel, unwilling to face the certainty of identity.

"It feeds on forgetting," Liv said. "But it dies from remembrance."

With a final blow, Astrid's axe split the specter's core. It shattered like glass. The village was saved. But only for a moment.

North of the fjord, in the gorge outside Skeldr Base, Erik Bloodaxe stood at the head of a shield wall of Warborn and Zepharian troops. The enemy had surrounded them with Voidborn swarms pouring from underground tunnels and darkened skyports alike.

Erik raised his axe, Stormfang, glimmering with lightning and fury.

"This is the line," he roared. "And they will not cross it."

And as the Voidborn came, he met them, not as myth, but as a man who would not break.

The gorge echoed with war cries and the screech of the unnatural. Erik Bloodaxe's voice thundered above it all, not words, but a howl, deep and ancient, pulled from the root of his soul. His warriors answered, pounding weapons to shields. Even the Zepharians, unused to such raw ferocity, felt something rise within them, a call older than language.

The Voidborn came in waves, shifting, faceless things with limbs like blades and skin that swallowed light. They flowed over the rocks and walls like water that meant to drown the earth.

Erik's shield slammed into the first wave, holding fast. Behind him, Gunnar flanked the breach, his warhammer humming with kinetic resonance.

"We're losing the west line!"

Erik snarled, turning mid-swing to drive his axe into the nearest creature's chest, if it could be called a chest. It shattered like wet glass.

"Then we push west."

"We'll be exposed!"

"Then we bleed like kings!"

He surged forward, smashing into the advancing line, carving a path one body at a time. Beside him, a Warborn named Skadi took a claw to the chest but didn't fall, she planted her spear and impaled two more before collapsing to her knees.

A Zepharian officer triggered a pulse barrier, slowing the Voidborn but at heavy energy cost.

"If this flank breaks, the central valley falls," he warned.

"Then it doesn't break," Erik snapped.

From the southern ridge, Astrid saw the battle unfold, just far enough to watch Erik fall. For a heartbeat, she thought he was gone. Then he rose again, axe slick, armor cracked, mouth open in a bloodied roar.

"I need a breach corridor to Erik now!" she shouted. "Divert skimmers and prep fire support!"

Rurik's voice crackled through her comm: "You'll be exposed. We don't have orbital cover!"

"Then we make our own."

She activated the sigils on her gauntlet, summoning a pillar of searing energy from Járnstóll's central relay.

"Flameborn, on me! We punch through or we die trying." And the ground between her and Erik turned to fire.

The gap between Astrid's ridge and Erik's battered line spanned less than a kilometer, but it may as well have been another world. The terrain was fractured, broken by Voidborn tunneling and electromagnetic destabilizers. Fires burned across collapsed bunkers, and the air shimmered with phase-disrupting pulses that bent time in uneven jolts.

"Eyes sharp," Astrid growled to her team. "These things distort more than light."

Her squad advanced in a V-formation, Warborn and Flameborn mixed, their weapons glowing with heated runes. Overhead, Zepharian skimmers laid down suppressive beams that disrupted rather than destroyed, breaking the quantum cohesion of Voidborn forms.

For the first time in days, Astrid saw fear on her people's faces, not of the enemy, but of what stood behind them.

"Ma'am," one of the younger warriors, Joren, said through clenched teeth, "we've got loyalist pockets radioing in. Human militias refusing to reinforce. They say this is your war, not theirs."

Astrid's breath caught.

"They think we caused the invasion? They think we brought it with us. That we woke the enemy."

Behind her, another soldier muttered, "They'd rather trust shadows than blood."

"That ends after today," Astrid snapped. "We hold this bridge. We save Erik. And then we remind the world what unity looks like."

They crested the final ridge, and chaos greeted them. Erik's position was down to a single circle of warriors. His cloak was in tatters, his helmet cracked, and Stormfang smoked with every breath. Around him lay Voidborn husks, half-dissolved into memory ash. He saw Astrid, and he grinned through blood.

"You took your time."

"You never wait for backup," she shot back, leaping into the fight.

Their lines converged, two halves reforged in fire. Steel sang. Void screamed. And the warriors of Midgard stood, if only for a little while, together.

The ridge trembled. Astrid and Erik stood back-to-back, their axes raised, surrounded by the warriors who had survived this long by sheer grit and faith in steel. Gunnar rejoined the front with bloodied fists, dragging a wounded Flameborn over his shoulder.

"They're regrouping," Rurik called from behind a rock shelf, fingers flying over a Zepharian tactical pad. "Something big is coming through."

Above them, the sky darkened, not with cloud, but with pressure, the air turning heavy with the weight of something vast, just beyond human comprehension.
The second wave had begun. And it was worse.

This time, the Voidborn did not come as individuals or swarms. They came as a single entity, a gestalt leviathan composed of what appeared to be thousands of smaller Voidborn bound together, limbs fused, memories chained. Its body twisted through the atmosphere like a serpent of grief and hunger.

"What the hell is that?" Liv shouted, blade raised.

"A war-mind," Rurik said, stunned. "They've adapted. That thing is coordinated. It thinks."

The leviathan screamed. And the world forgot how to breathe. Entire squads dropped to their knees. Some screamed names of dead loved ones. Others clutched their heads, begging for the memories to stop. A Warborn named Brynja collapsed, whispering, "I was never real. I was never..."

"Anchor them!" Astrid shouted. "Light your runes—remember who you are!"

Liv gritted her teeth and plunged her frostblade into the ground. "We need reinforcements."

Erik raised a fist to the sky, the Zepharian beacon on his gauntlet glowing crimson.

"Then call them," he said.

From above, the sky cracked, not with Voidborn, but with fire. Drakenskip reinforcements, piloted by Valkari and Flameborn, descended in arcs of lightning and flame. Earth's fractured resistance had heard the call. The lines held—barely. But the war-mind was still coming. And it remembered everything they had ever feared.

The war-mind descended like an avalanche of void. Its mass shifted constantly, arms appearing and disappearing, faces forming in the swirl of its body like memories caught in a storm. Each step it took consumed the terrain beneath it. Where it passed, reality folded. Trees twisted into bone. Ruins reconstructed themselves into impossible geometries, half-flesh and half-forgotten.

Rurik yelled over the roar: "That thing isn't just attacking—it's rewriting! If it reaches Járnstóll, we lose the Earth lattice!"

"Then we stop it now," Astrid snapped.

She turned to Erik.

"We go inside. Strike the war-core directly. The Zepharians said their gestalt minds need anchors."

"You're saying it has a brain?"

"I'm saying it has a heart. And we crush it."

Erik nodded. "As we did at the gates of Skeldr."

"Only with higher stakes," Liv muttered.

Gunnar clapped a hand on Astrid's shoulder. "We doing this with style?"

She smirked. "We're doing it with fury."

They charged. The strike team raced across a battlefield melting under their feet, dodging spectral limbs and waves of thought-static that tried to force doubt into their minds. One Flameborn was caught mid-run, frozen in place as the war-mind projected a false memory, her child, smiling from beneath the rubble. She never screamed. Astrid led the way, axe blazing.

"Focus! Anchor! Don't believe the ghosts!"

A tendril of shadow lashed toward Erik. He caught it mid-swing, severing it clean.

"Not today, filth!"

They reached the war-mind's base, a roiling mass of pulsing dark tissue, carved with symbols in reversed Norse, meanings meant to unmake meaning itself.

"This is where we make it bleed," Astrid growled.

"Or die trying," Liv said, eyes glowing with activated sigils.

"Either way," Erik said, gripping Stormfang, "they'll remember our fire."

And they leapt into the storm.

Crossing the threshold was like stepping into a dream made of ruin. The war-mind's interior was not made of flesh or metal, but memory, stolen, shattered, repurposed. Walls pulsed with flickers of childhoods long lost, battles half-remembered, regrets replayed on repeat. The ground was shifting ash, occasionally resolving into stone, bone, or forgotten faces.

Astrid landed first, her boots skidding across a floor that refused to settle. Her axe dimmed, the runes flickering.

"It's trying to erase our sense of time," she said. "Don't trust what you see. Or what you remember seeing."

Behind her, Erik dropped into the core chamber like a thunderclap. He took two steps and froze—eyes wide.

"Hell," he whispered. "It's my brothers…"

He saw them, Halvard and Bjorn, standing at the edge of the field, armored in fur and steel, smiling as they had in the days before Ragnarok.

"You failed us," they said together, lips unmoving.

"You chose the stars instead of home."

He raised his axe, but his hands trembled.

Astrid grabbed his arm. "They're not real."

"I know," he growled, blinking hard. "But I feel them."

Liv stepped into the light, and her dead Flameborn mentor appeared before her, eyes hollow.

"You're a weapon," it said. "You always were."

She screamed and hurled a blade into the mirage,it shattered into glass, dissolving into screams.

"Strike forward!" she yelled. "The core is ahead! It wants us to spiral inward!"

The terrain shifted again, the air filling with dissonant chants, echoes of old Norse prayers, corrupted, bent backward. Each word tried to peel back the soul.

Gunnar fell to his knees. "I can't... I'm not who I thought I was..."

Rurik grabbed him by the collar. "Then be who you are now!"

Ahead, a tower formed from writhing threads of thought. At its center: the war-mind's neural spine.

"There!" Astrid shouted.

"If we break it—"

"We weaken it. That's all," she said. "This war doesn't end here. But we can remind it we're still standing."

And they charged the core, not with certainty—but with flame.

The tower of thought-flesh loomed like a monument to extinction. It wasn't solid. It wasn't even entirely real. But the war-mind's neural spine pulsed with rhythm, an echo of consciousness. One the Voidborn had shaped into a weapon. A mind not meant to think, but to suppress thought itself.

Rurik tapped into his Zepharian interface, feeding commands into the surrounding reality.

"I can weaken its lattice. Drop its guard for ten seconds."

"Ten will do," Astrid said, gripping her axe.

"We'll only get one shot," Liv added. "If we miss—"

"Then we die as sparks in the dark," Erik finished.

The neural tower opened like a blooming wound. At its heart: a singularity of hunger, a knot of writhing voidcode tangled with dying memories—some human, some not. It wasn't just defending itself. It was trying to make them part of it. The tower roared.

Astrid ran first, hurling herself through waves of phantasmal fire and collapsing timelines. She slammed her axe into the spine's edge, and the runes along its blade howled as they met resistance deeper than metal.

Liv threw both of her frostblades, piercing secondary nodes. Gunnar took a hit from a lashing tentacle, his chestplate caving, but still he rose, wielding a two-handed hammer of pure kinetic rune-force.

"Rurik!" Astrid shouted. "Now!"

Rurik triggered the overload. The chamber screamed. For a moment, everyone saw everything. Their childhoods. Their deaths. Their victories. The day the stars burned. The day Midgard died. The day it rose again. And then the core cracked.

"Out!" Astrid barked.

The group turned and ran, gravity twisting, time lagging. Rurik stumbled, but Liv grabbed his wrist, dragging him as the tower folded behind them.

They erupted into daylight. The war-mind reeled, its body fragmenting in the sky, bellowing not in pain, but in shock. It hadn't expected resistance. Not like this.

It retreated, breaking apart into smaller swarms that scattered across the planet like wounded gods. They had not destroyed it. But they had made it bleed.

Smoke curled from the valley. Ash drifted like black snow, settling onto ruined bunkers, broken Drakenskip hulls, and scorched Zepharian gunports. The sky was clearing—not with victory, but with the momentary quiet that follows a storm too large to name.

Astrid stood on a crag overlooking the battlefield. Her armor was cracked. Her left gauntlet hung in tatters. Her face was smeared with sweat, blood, and memory. But she was alive. Below, Erik Bloodaxe knelt beside a fallen Warborn, placing the soldier's axe across their chest in silence. He did not speak, did not weep. He simply stood when the ritual was done and nodded once to Astrid.

"We won?" Liv asked behind her, voice raspy.

Astrid didn't answer at first.

"We endured," she said finally. "And we hurt them."

Rurik approached with his datapad. "Confirmed signal disruption across the planetary net. The war-mind fractured. But its pieces... they're already regrouping."

Astrid closed her eyes. "They'll come back stronger."

"And next time?" Liv asked.

"We'll be ready," Astrid said. "Because now we've seen their mind. And they've seen ours."

High above, the auroras returned, this time untouched by darkness, at least for a while. They danced green and gold across the sky, watched by warriors, civilians, and Zepharians alike.

The people of Earth, divided by culture, belief, and blood, stood under the same light again. But far beyond the moon, in the dark places between stars, the Svarthjarta watched. And they were learning.

Chapter 16: The Voidborn War

There was no sensation of movement. Only transition. As the Warborn ships passed through the rift, the physical rules that once governed their understanding of reality dissolved. It wasn't darkness that greeted them, it was absence. An absence so complete, even thought resisted forming.

Inside the lead Drakenskip, the Hjartstorm, silence reigned. Astrid stood at the observation ring, her breath fogging the glass despite the ship's environmental controls. The Riftspace beyond was… wrong. Not empty. Not black. It was an inverted potential, a realm stripped of anchoring time. Light moved like water. Stars flickered and vanished before they were born.

"Confirming passage," Leif's voice crackled through the ship-wide intercom, filtered and distorted. "We're inside."

"Inside what?" Yrsa muttered from the weapons bay. "This place doesn't want us here."

Erik stood beside Astrid, his arms crossed, his armor humming quietly as the Eidrsigil on his back reacted to the environment. The runes on his gauntlet pulsed in erratic rhythm.

"What is this place?" he asked quietly.

Astrid didn't answer right away. Her mind, enhanced by the Hjartablóð, was attempting to process not just images, but conceptual architecture. This realm didn't have geography. It had intent.

"It's not a dimension," she said. "It's an awareness. We're inside the Svarthjarta's periphery. Not its core. Not yet. This is where it watches. Where it waits."

No sooner had she spoken than the alarms flared. Proximity sensors spiked. Not with objects, but with gravitational irregularities. Ripples in space folded inward like craters collapsing in reverse.

"Incoming!" shouted Hakon. "Movement on all axes!"

The viewscreen flickered, then stabilized to reveal shapes. At first, they resembled creatures: long, spined forms made of obsidian-black light and trailing tendrils of electric hunger. But the longer one stared at them, the more they unraveled, as if the mind refused to fully comprehend them.

"Voidborn," Erik growled. "The Svarthjarta's vanguard."

Astrid locked her bracer and activated the ship's outer defensive runes. "No, not just vanguard. These are scouts, designed to read us, adapt, and relay what we are."

"Then let's make sure they get the wrong impression," Yrsa said, slamming her fist into the weapons console.

Hjartstorm's side turrets erupted with a volley of plasma-rune bolts. The energy sliced through one of the Voidborn, which exploded in a bloom of distortion and shattered light.

Another dove straight through the hull, phasing through the outer wall like mist and reappearing inside the aft deck. Screams echoed through the halls.

Erik was already moving, axe in hand. Astrid followed, activating her bracer's light-forged blade. When they reached the breach, the creature was tearing through the air, tendrils dragging the weight of gravity itself. The air stank of ozone and unformed sound.

Erik hurled his axe through its core. It didn't die. It folded.

Astrid stepped forward, runes flaring from her wrist, and spoke a phrase she had never learned but always known.

"Vakna úr myrkri."
Awaken from darkness.

The light struck true. The Voidborn screamed, not in sound, but in raw dissonance, and evaporated into threads of broken futures. The breach sealed.

The breach was sealed. The voidborn scout was gone. But no one aboard Hjartstorm relaxed. The rift wasn't just reacting to their presence. It was studying them, responding to them like a living immune system identifying a threat.

"Shields are holding," Leif called from the navigation core.

"But the laws of physics are degrading. We're running on predictive probability more than inertia."

Yrsa groaned. "I swear, if you say that in human words again, I'll kiss you just to shut you up."

Leif turned bright red. "I—I just mean we don't know what's real anymore."

Erik stood over the Eidrsigil core. It pulsed like a heartbeat.

"We need to find a place to deploy this."

"Where?" Astrid asked. "This realm doesn't have a center."

"No," said Runa, emerging from her meditative trance. "But it has a throat."

The Warborn fleet shifted direction, drawn toward a gravitational sink, a collapse of possibility that twisted the sky into a spiral. Around it floated debris: not asteroids, but ruins.

Erik leaned forward, his eyes narrowing.

"That's a city."

And it was. Floating like an island torn from the surface of a long-dead planet, it spun slowly in the rift's rotation— buildings of crystal and alloy, towers shaped like spires of music and math. A civilization once great, now frozen in timeless decay.

They passed another, less elegant, more brutalist. Charred banners still clung to broken parapets. Bones drifted like pollen.

"How many civilizations?" Astrid whispered. "How many almost became something more?"

Runa's voice trembled. "These are the fallen. The possible made impossible."

As they drifted near the third ruin, one composed of black monoliths and spiraling paths, the Eidrsigil flared.

Leif nearly dropped his console. "We're receiving a signal. Non-verbal. Emotional."

Astrid tuned in. A sensation passed through her, not thought, not language. It was envy. The kind that festered across lifetimes. Not of power. Not of wealth. Of potential.

The Svarthjarta was watching. And it hated them—not for what they were, but for what they might become.

"It doesn't fear us because we're strong," she whispered. "It fears what we could be."

The Warborn landed at the edge of the broken crystal city, deploying a forward team: Astrid, Erik, Yrsa, Leif, and two elite Awakened—Galen Veir and Saska Runechild.

The structures were still warm. Not physically, but metaphysically, like someone had tried to hold onto this place, long after it had fallen. Glyphs flickered along the walls, reacting to their presence.

"Zepharian derivative," Leif said. "But evolved. These people were more advanced than the Zepharians."

Astrid ran her hand along a console, and it lit beneath her touch. A voice echoed, not in her mind, but through the material of the building itself.

"We reached too far. We rose too fast. We became a flame, and the void drinks fire."

Yrsa drew her blade. "It's a grave."

Astrid shook her head. "No. It's a warning."

Suddenly, the light above them flickered—and a shape descended. Not a creature. Not even a ship. A mask.

Ten stories tall. Carved from a material that devoured light. Featureless except for a single vertical slit of white fire.

Erik's axe spun into his hand. "Is that the Svarthjarta?"

"No," Astrid said, her voice shaking. "It's its voice."

The mask opened. And the sky screamed.

The mask opened. And the void screamed.

No sound issued from it. No sonic wave, no physical force.
But every Warborn in the city dropped to a knee or
collapsed to the ground, clutching their heads, as a psychic
roar tore through their minds.

Erik staggered, one gauntleted hand pressed to his temple.
His breath came in short, violent gasps. The Eidrsigil pulsed
wildly on his back. Astrid fell to one knee, her fingers
clawing at the crystal floor. Her vision blurred, not from
pain, but from *dissonance*.

The scream wasn't a message. It was a cancellation. A direct
assault on will, identity, belief, an attempt to flatten their
consciousness into silence.

"It's trying to unravel us," she gasped. "To make us stop
becoming."

Yrsa, standing through sheer force of rage, howled into the
sky. "Not today!"

She hurled her axe, not to destroy, but to mark. The spinning
blade struck the ground just beneath the mask and
embedded itself deep, igniting a pulse of runes that crackled
outward like wildfire. The scream ceased. Not entirely.
But enough.

The air folded like broken glass, and from the split between
realms emerged a being. Not the Svarthjarta. But its limb.

It was humanoid only in shape. A titan of swirling darkness,
runed like a perverse parody of the Warborn, with armor of
folded voidlight and eyes that shone like inverted stars.

"Astrid," Erik shouted. "The Eidrsigil—now!"

But she wasn't moving. She was seeing.

In the presence of the entity, the Hjartablóð flared uncontrollably. Astrid's mind spiraled into a flash of futures:

> A world scorched and gray, where no new songs were written.

> Children born silent, never dreaming.

> The stars themselves flickering out—not dead, but irrelevant.

The Svarthjarta didn't destroy through violence. It froze. It interrupted. It ended momentum.

"Kill the future," it whispered in every language.

And yet there was a flicker. A path. If the Eidrsigil could anchor becoming, could declare that evolution would continue, the entity would be forced into a form. And forms could be broken.

The titanic limb struck the ground with a blow that sent shockwaves through the city. One of the Drakenskip, anchored above, shuddered under the blast, losing altitude. Erik charged, runes blazing. His axe met the creature's blade, if it could be called that. A weapon formed from compressed despair and extinguished stars. Sparks of unreality sprayed across the battlefield. Yrsa followed, blade singing.

Galen and Saska unleashed rune-bursts, shaping explosions into jagged spears of crystallized possibility. The creature stumbled, not from pain, but from confusion. It didn't understand resistance. It had never been fought like this.

Astrid rose, her legs trembling, and pulled the Eidrsigil from its housing. It glowed now with more than stored memory.

It shimmered with every Warborn's choice, every step they'd taken toward something more. She sprinted toward the center of the collapse, where the mask hovered above the battlefield.

"Cover me!" she shouted.

Leif, now aboard Hjartstorm, initiated an orbital rune burst. Runes traced the skies, flaring as they formed a protective spiral around her. The creature tried to intercept, but Erik launched himself onto its shoulder, burying his axe deep into its neck.

"NOW!" he roared.

Astrid dove into the pit below the mask. And slammed the Eidrsigil into the broken heart of the rift.

Light erupted in all directions—silver, blue, crimson, gold. Not destructive, but formative. The Svarthjarta's realm convulsed. The air stilled. Time pressed itself into alignment, like water freezing into place. For the first time, the Svarthjarta had to occupy defined space. It had to play by rules. And it was furious.

The mask shattered, releasing a keening cry that split the city's remnants apart. The void titan reeled backward, limbs curling in on itself. Astrid collapsed near the sigil, barely breathing. Erik ran to her, catching her before she hit the ground.

"You did it," he said, voice rough.

"No," she whispered. "We did."

Above them, the sky flared open. And the real battle began.

The rift reacted violently.

Where once the Svarthjarta's realm had felt infinite, fluid, and unshaped, it now buckled under the pressure of definition. The Eidrsigil's anchoring effect spread like a root system through the collapsed remnants of past civilizations, stitching together laws of space, time, and cause.

"Stabilization field holding!" Leif shouted through comms. "But they're coming."

And they were. From every direction, the Voidborn swarmed, hundreds of shapes, each unique, each a mockery of form. One resembled a headless dragon with wings of ink; another crawled along geometry that didn't exist; a third howled with the stolen voices of ancient kings.

The Warborn formed a ring around the Eidrsigil. Yrsa stood front and center, twin axes coated in silver flame.

"No one touches the core," she growled.

Galen raised a gravity pulse barrier. Saska flicked runes into the air with her fingers, constructing sigils that spun like sawblades. Even the wounded stood.

They didn't hold the line because they believed they could survive. They held it because some things had to be protected, no matter the cost.

And then, it came. The sky opened with a terrible *stillness*. Not noise. Not silence. The *removal* of motion itself. The air turned cold, not with temperature, but with disinterest.

A shape descended, massive, humanoid, yet shifting, its form an abstraction of will, cloaked in veils of unreality. It had no face, only a fracture, a crack in space where a head should be. Stars fell into it, and never returned.

"That's it," Astrid whispered. "The Core."

The Svarthjarta had shown itself, not fully, but enough.
It stepped onto the field of becoming. And it was *wrong*.

Erik stepped forward, runes blazing down his arms, the
Hjartablóð fused into his skin now, the last weapon they
could trust. He raised his voice—not loud, but absolute.

"You wanted to stop us from becoming."
"Then come see what we are."

The battle that followed could not be sung. There were no
horns. No shields breaking. No mud beneath their boots.
There was only light and will. Erik met the Svarthjarta in the
center of the collapse, where the laws of physics stuttered
and tried to write themselves anew with every second. His
axe burned with potential—every choice he had ever made,
every moment where he might have given up and hadn't.

Astrid backed him with energy pulses, projecting harmonic
frequencies into the Svarthjarta's structure, forcing it to
resolve. Leif activated the Eidrsigil's second core—
broadcasting becoming as a waveform. The Svarthjarta
roared. Not in rage. Not in fear. In recognition.

It knew now what they were. And that meant it had to
destroy them, right now, before they spread. It lunged.
Erik struck. And for a moment, the Svarthjarta felt pain.

But even as they drove it back, they knew... It could not be
destroyed here. Not fully. Only banished. Only contained.

Erik turned to Astrid.

"You have to finish the core alignment. Lock the rift from
both sides."

"But that means—"

"I know."

He smiled. And for a brief moment, he looked not like a king, not like a warlord... But like the boy who once sailed through storm-churned fjords with nothing but a name and a blade.

"If this is the cost of our becoming..."

He raised his axe.

"Then let me pay it."

Astrid nodded, tears blazing in her silver-lit eyes. "I'll make them remember."

"No," Erik said. "Make them continue."

He turned. And ran straight into the Svarthjarta.

The Eidrsigil flared white. The rift screamed. And everything vanished. Except the flame.

Epilogue: The Flame That Remains

One Year Later

The world remembered him. Not as a king. Not as a conqueror. But as a man who walked into the fire, not to destroy, but to preserve what could be.

Erik Bloodaxe had died where no man had ever lived, inside the riftheart of the Svarthjarta, a place beyond time, beyond form, beyond reason. His axe had struck the impossible, not to win, but to *become* the final act of defiance.

The Eidrsigil, anchored in his hands, had not shattered. It had ignited. The flame of becoming had not been extinguished. It had been carried.

Peace did not come easily.

The riftstorms didn't vanish overnight. Remnants of the Voidborn still crawled through the dark spaces between dimensions, requiring vigilance and strength to contain. Earth, scarred and humbled, stood on the edge of a new era. But they had Astrid. She had survived.

She was scarred, changed and her eyes permanently ringed with silver light, her arm fused with Hjartablóð, but alive. She emerged from the breach with Erik's axe strapped to her back and the fractured Eidrsigil cradled in her arms. And she spoke not of vengeance, nor of sorrow. Only of legacy.

A new council formed named The Flameguard, composed of Awakened leaders, Earth officials, and Zepharian envoys. It was not perfect. Nothing built from ash ever is. But it held.

The Warborn Temples, once myth, now rebuilt as centers for training and peacekeeping, sprouted across continents. Children of all bloodlines studied side by side, learning the old runes and the new sciences.

Statues were raised not just to Erik, but to the fallen.

Yrsa the Boundless
Runa the Seer
Galen Veir and Saska Runechild

And countless others who'd stood at the edge of the void
and held the line

Yet above them all, one name was etched in runes brighter
than flame:

Erik Bloodaxe
Last King of the Old World. First Flame of the New.

Astrid refused any crown. She became something else: a
guardian of flame. She walked the ruins of old cities and the
halls of orbital stations. She taught. She listened. She lit
fires, not of war, but of purpose.

Every year, on the anniversary of the final battle, she
returned to the place where she had come through the rift.
She placed a single object upon the shrine stone:

Erik's axe.

She would not wield it again. It belonged to the past.
But the flame it kindled, that lived in her eyes, in her voice,
in the generations that followed.

Sometimes, in the quiet between stars, Zepharian sensors
picked up something strange. Not a rift. Not a scream. A
whisper. A hum. Like the resonance of a name echoing
through the structure of reality. And Astrid would smile, just
slightly, when the signal reached her.

"Still watching?" she'd murmur to the wind. "I hope you're
proud."

A new order emerged, not empire, not dynasty. A culture.
They called themselves the Flamekind. Not because they
wielded fire. But because they had carried it.

Erik's sacrifice had not ended the threat and had bought
time, space, hope. Astrid's survival ensured that spark
became a blaze. The children born in the years after the war
were different. Some had eyes that shimmered with runes.
Some dreamed in songs they'd never heard.

And when they played, they built things, small things,
strange things, out of scrap and light and stories. One child,
when asked what they wanted to be, answered simply:

"More."

And the teachers nodded. Because they understood.

In Ydalir's rebuilt high chamber, a sculpture stood behind
the hearth. It was simple. Black stone, runed with silver, its
surface split by a single red-orange seam that glowed gently,
eternally. No plaque. No name. But everyone knew what it
was.

The Flame That Remains.

And those who stood beforeit, young and old, Flamekind
and otherwise, would sometimes feel something stir in their
chest. Not grief. Not fear. Not sorrow. But fire.

The End

Appendixes:

Appendix 1: Character Profiles

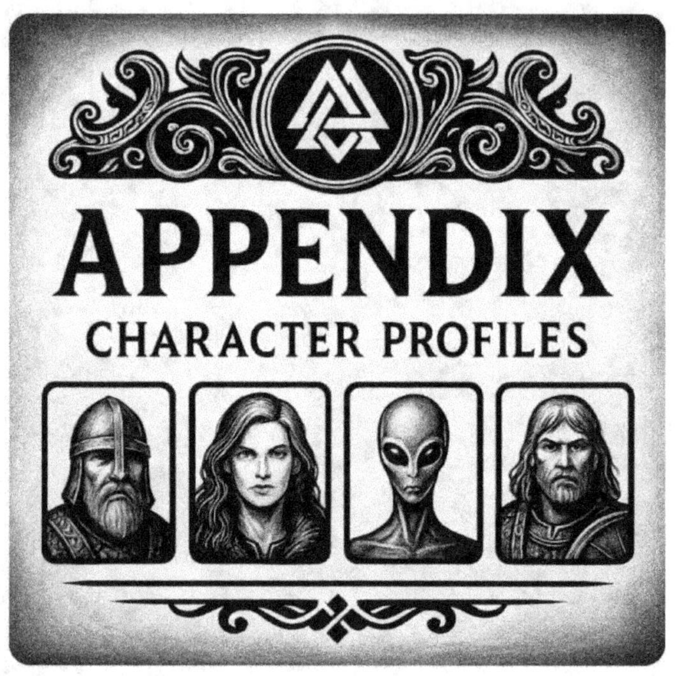

Erik Bloodaxe

Aliases:	King of the North, The Storm-Axe, Warlord of the Stars
Role:	Viking chieftain and first commander of the Drakenskip
Affiliation:	Norse, Flameborn, Human-Viking Alliance
Origin:	Fjords of Norway, 9th Century
Traits:	Commanding, visionary, tactically brutal
Equipment:	Stormfang (rune-infused battle axe), hybrid Zepharian-Viking armor, resonance shield
Arc Highlights:	First contact with the Zepharians Led humanity's initial off-world expansion Survived the first Voidborn breach Acts as a moral compass between old Norse honor and galactic futurism
Personality:	Stoic and relentless, but driven by deep loyalty to his kin

Astrid Jorgensen

Aliases:	The Runeborn, Flamekeeper, Seer of Earth
Role:	Modern historian turned warrior-leader
Affiliation:	Flameborn, Earth Resistance
Origin:	Tromsø, Norway (21st Century)
Traits:	Highly intelligent, emotionally intuitive, fiercely determined
Equipment:	Zepharian neural-grafted armor, rune-forged axe, Járnstóll command sigil
Arc Highlights:	First human descendant to awaken post-Drakenskip DNA Bridge between scientific reasoning and ancestral belief Instrumental in decoding Zepharian memory anchors
Personality:	Analytical under pressure, spiritual when alone, driven by legacy and truth

Torvald the Elder

Aliases:	The Skeptic, Old Iron
Role:	Veteran warrior and Erik's longtime second
Affiliation:	Norse Drakenskip crew
Origin:	Trondheim region, 9th Century
Traits:	Skeptical, blunt, deeply honorable
Equipment:	Ancestral broadsword, frost-threaded chainmail
Arc Highlights:	One of the few to question the Zepharians openly Fought alongside Erik in the early campaigns Ultimately dies saving a group of hybrid children from a Voidborn incursion
Personality:	Grim humor, mistrustful of change, fiercely loyal

Gunnar the Red

Aliases:	The Ember-Fist, Youngblood
Role:	Viking warrior with unmatched physical strength
Affiliation:	Warborn, frontline shock troops
Origin:	Born during the last Norse raiding era
Traits:	Reckless, charismatic, unpredictable
Equipment:	Rune-charged war gauntlets, Zepharian-enhanced musculature
Arc Highlights:	Early zealot turned disciplined soldier Rescued Flameborn captives in the breach of Skeldr Conflict with Astrid's diplomacy-first approach
Personality:	Brash, impulsive, grows into leadership

Zepharian Prime (Unnamed Leader)

Aliases:	The Observer, Voice of the Star-Forge
Role:	Lead emissary of the Zepharian High Council
Affiliation:	Zepharians
Origin:	Aru-Ven orbital core, Zepharian domain
Traits:	Calculating, serene, ancient knowledge-bearer
Equipment:	Light-form robes, translation crystal array, memory core staff
Arc Highlights:	Initiated First Contact Attempted to suppress human emotion-based strategies Sacrificed part of its own consciousness to stabilize the Flameborn fusion process
Personality:	Alien calm, struggles to grasp human emotion, deeply invested in cosmic balance

Liv Skjoldr

Aliases:	Ice Fang, Flameborn Shadow
Role:	Elite recon operative and personal guard to Astrid
Affiliation:	Flameborn
Origin:	Hidden village near Svalbard, raised in exile
Traits:	Deadly precise, fiercely protective, emotionally restrained
Equipment:	Dual frostblades, adaptive stealth mesh armor, runic grappling gauntlet
Arc Highlights:	First to kill a Voidborn using hybrid Flameborn weaponry Rescued Astrid during the siege of Freyja's Gate In a crisis of identity after Flameborn were labeled inhuman by resistance cells

Rurik Halvarsson

Aliases:	The Engineer of Flame, Forge-Mind
Role:	Zepharian-tech integrator and tactical systems specialist
Affiliation:	Flameborn, Járnstóll Defense Core
Origin:	Oslo, technocrat caste
Traits:	Brilliant, sarcastic, and impatient with warriors
Equipment:	Neural-linked forgeband, exo-spine processor, data-spike array
Arc Highlights:	Created Earth's first functioning anti-Void lattice node Mentored several younger warriors, including Joren and Brynja Sacrifices a portion of his neural integrity to stabilize the Drakenskip reactor
Personality:	Analytical, deeply cynical, cracks under emotional pressure

Freydis Vangir

Aliases:	The Blade of Blood, Purifier
Role:	Rogue Warborn leader and rival to Astrid
Affiliation:	Breakaway faction of Warborn loyalists
Origin:	Icelandic Norse revivalist enclave
Traits:	Rigid, militant, traditionalist
Equipment:	Runic greatblade, symbiotic armor, memory-excision talon
Arc Highlights:	Believes integration with Zepharian culture is a betrayal of Viking honor Challenges Astrid in a ritual duel before the All-Thing Later offers reluctant alliance during the war-mind breach
Personality:	Cold, proud, but ultimately cares about Earth's survival

Brynja Thorsdottir

Aliases:	The Iron Hearth
Role:	Frontline defender and spiritual symbol of human-Flameborn unity
Affiliation:	Warborn, Valkari auxiliary
Origin:	Drakenskip-born generation
Traits:	Compassionate, fearless, devoted to the old gods and new flame
Equipment:	Kinetic shield-array, hybrid frostmail, flame-totem pendant
Arc Highlights:	Defended the last refugee line during the collapse of Bifrost Station Her death at the hands of the war-mind became a turning point in unity
Personality:	Warm, deeply spiritual, seen as a martyr by many

The War-Mind (Svarthjarta Sub-core)

Aliases:	The Voice That Devours, The Mirror of Grief
Role:	Sentient weapon of the Voidborn swarm
Affiliation:	Svarthjarta
Origin:	Unknown—possibly a fractured soul construct
Traits:	Adaptive, telepathic, impossible to fully perceive
Equipment:	Uses memories as weapons, feeds on cognitive dissonance
Arc Highlights:	Breached Midgard's defense lattice during the Battle of the Spine Fought and wounded Astrid within the neural core Currently regrouping and learning faster from each failed encounter
Personality:	Alien and unknowable, mimics emotions but does not feel

Appendix II: Technology Guide

Technology Guide

Drakenskip

- Classification: Hybrid Starcraft / Warship

- Origin: Joint design—Zepharian frame, Norse symbolism and bio-input control

- Function: Long-range interstellar transport and combat vessel

- Capabilities:

  - Runes react to genetic markers of Viking descendants

  - Can traverse subspace using memory-synced navigation

  - Self-repairing nanostructure hull

- Key Appearances: Chapter 3, 6, 12

- Notes: Considered a sacred relic by the Flameborn. Its core sings in Old Norse when activated by descendants.

Járnstóll

- Classification: Command Nexus / Tactical Interface

- Origin: Zepharian superstructure converted for human use

- Function: Serves as a war command hub and interface with galactic communications

- Capabilities:

    - Neural mapping of commanders

    - Tactical modeling based on myth-memory resonance

    - Stores battle simulations drawn from Viking saga structure

- Key Appearances: Chapters 7, 9

- Notes: Only Astrid and Erik could fully interface with Járnstóll due to lineage.

Voidborn War-Mind Shard

- Classification: Cognitive weapon / Corruption virus

- Origin: Unknown; presumed non-physical consciousness graft

- Function: Infects memory, destabilizes identity

- Capabilities:

    - Feeds on fear, doubt, legacy disruptions

    - Can rewrite sensory input

    - Has no physical form, but manifests through shadows and glitches in reality

- Key Appearances: Chapters 9, 12, 16

- Notes: Possibly sentient. Astrid's neural resistance was the only effective defense.

Flameborn Gauntlets

- Classification: Personal combat enhancer

- Origin: Modified Viking armaments with Zepharian tech core

- Function: Enhances grip strength, shock delivery, and energy deflection

- Capabilities:

    - Energy pulses triggered by battle cry

    - Heat-reactive to anger, amplifying blows

- Key Appearances: Gunnar's signature gear

- Notes: Only usable by activated descendants.

Zepharian Memory Anchors

- Classification: Quantum data storage / Historical recorder

- Origin: Zepharian ancestral archiving devices

- Function: Preserve and project historical memory

- Capabilities:

    - Replay past events in full sensory simulation

- - Project memories into open space via psionic waves

- Key Appearances: Chapters 2, 5

- Notes: Required to reveal the original disappearance of the Norsemen.

Bifrost Gate Relay

- Classification: Planetary Portal / Subspace Network Node

- Origin: Zepharian-Viking co-engineered

- Function: Allows instantaneous travel between planetary systems

- Capabilities:

    - Rune-coded access sequence

    - Powered by memory resonance

    - Can be overloaded to cause starburst implosion

- Key Appearances: Chapter 10, 12

- Notes: Only active during high solar flare intervals. Believed to have mythological connection to Norse Bifröst.

Runeskin Implants

- Classification: Bio-cybernetic Interface

- Origin: Zepharian neural-glyph fusion

- Function: Enhances physical reflexes, memory retention, and ancestry unlocking

- Capabilities:

  - Allows interaction with Zepharian tech

  - Glows in response to psionic proximity

  - Can be hacked by Voidborn frequencies

- Key Appearances: Chapter 6, 8

- Notes: Activation causes hallucinations of ancestral visions.

Svarthjarta Pulse Spines

- Classification: Biological Weapon / Psychic Disruptor

- Origin: Grown inside Voidborn monstrosities

- Function: Emits chaos frequencies that destabilize cognitive cohesion

- Capabilities:

  - Disrupts Flameborn synaptic control

  - Can tear through material and memory layers

- Key Appearances: Chapter 9, 13

- Notes: Banned from study by Zepharians due to mental contamination risk.

Forge-Stones of Járnstóll

- Classification: Energy Core / Modular AI Forge

- Origin: Zepharian inner sanctum

- Function: Produces custom tools, weapons, and armor through memory-keyed construction

- Capabilities:

    o Responds to emotional signatures

    o Can adapt mid-battle to user needs

- Key Appearances: Chapter 11, 14

- Notes: Considered sacred—each Viking has one embedded in their armor during forging rites.

Mjölnar Protocol Satellites

- Classification: Orbital Defense Grid

- Origin: Human-designed, Zepharian-enhanced

- Function: Defends Earth using energy-based kinetic lances

- Capabilities:

    o Uses storm energy as ammunition

- - - o   Requires dual-authentication from Flameborn

- Key Appearances: Chapter 12

- Notes: A nod to Thor's hammer. Their activation is a last-resort defense measure.

Appendix III: Faction Codex

The Flameborn

- Type: Hybrid Warrior Society

- Origin: Descendants of Viking lineage enhanced by Zepharian bio-seeds

- Beliefs: Fire and memory are sacred; strength through transformation

- Structure: Clan-based; led by Astrid Jorgensen as Flamekeeper

- Key Figures: Astrid, Liv Skjoldr, Brynja

- Allies: Zepharians, Earth Resistance

- Enemies: Voidborn, Warborn extremists

- Notables: Defenders of the memory core during the Voidborn breach; creators of the Forgeborn flame-tech

---

The Zepharians

- Type: Post-organic Alien Civilization

- Origin: Star system near Aru-Ven, older than Earth's recorded history

- Beliefs: Evolution through wisdom, preservation of ancestral memory

- Structure: Council of Echoes (collective memory hive)

- Key Figures: Zepharian Prime, the Witness, Archivist Theta

- Allies: Flameborn, Astrid

- Enemies: Svarthjarta

- Notables: Provided the Drakenskip and seeded Earth's Norse ancestors with bio-tech markers

---

The Warborn

- Type: Rogue Military Faction

- Origin: Norse hybrid splinter sect

- Beliefs: Power through conquest, purity of Viking bloodlines

- Structure: Martial hierarchy under warlords

- Key Figures: Freydis Vangir, Gunnar (former)

- Allies: None currently

- Enemies: Flameborn, Zepharians

- Notables: Attempted coup during All-Thing Reclamation; used corrupted Voidborn weapons

---

The Voidborn / Svarthjarta

- Type: Cosmic Antagonists / Devourers of Legacy

- Origin: Unknown, believed to exist outside known time

- Beliefs: Nothingness is the natural state of the universe

- Structure: Hive of autonomous horrors ruled by the Black Heart

- Key Figures: War-Mind, The Mirror, The Pale King

- Allies: None

- Enemies: All memory-based life

- Notables: Responsible for the collapse of the Zepharian outer colonies and the Rift Siege

---

The Valkari

- Type: Cultural Priesthood and Diplomatic Order

- Origin: Flameborn and traditional Norse lineage

- Beliefs: Honor, ancestry, unity between past and future

- Structure: Elders and emissaries, ritual-led

- Key Figures: Brynja Thorsdottir, Elder Eisa

- Allies: Flameborn, Resistance

- Enemies: Warborn extremists, Voidborn

- Notables: Maintained the ritual balance during hybridization, creators of the Memory-Rune Codex

Appendix IV: Glossary of Terms

Glossary

All-Thing

- Pronunciation: *ahl-ting*

- Definition: The great gathering or council of Norse-descended clans and hybrid factions.

- Context: Reclaimed as a unifying ritual in the modern interstellar age; critical events in Chapters 7 and 11.

Bifrost Gate

- Definition: A memory-reactive interstellar portal station.

- Context: Used for transit between distant strongholds; partially mythologized in Norse culture.

Bloodbond

- Definition: A ritual link between two Flameborn warriors that allows them to share senses and power during combat.

- Context: Rarely performed due to the mental risks; Gunnar and Brynja performed one in Chapter 12.

The Breach

- Definition: A cataclysmic event during which the Voidborn accessed Earth's upper atmosphere and memory grid.

- Context: Central conflict of Chapter 10, where multiple factions are tested.

Drakenskip

- Pronunciation: *drah-ken-skip*

- Definition: The legendary hybrid ship built from Viking lore and Zepharian tech.

- Context: Used for travel across space, tied to genetic lineages.

Echo Strain

- Definition: A genetic anomaly passed down by Viking bloodlines, allowing telepathic communication and memory recall.

- Context: Triggered by Flameborn awakening; basis for many of Astrid's early visions.

Flameborn

- Definition: A faction of awakened Viking descendants imbued with Zepharian enhancements.

- Context: They serve as elite warriors and spiritual successors of Erik's vision.

Forge-Stone

- Definition: A small crystalline artifact implanted into warriors during their coming-of-age ritual.

- Context: Reacts to battle-readiness and emotional triggers; each is unique to its bearer.

Járnstóll

- Pronunciation: *yarn-stohl*

- Definition: The Zepharian-forged command and strategy core.

- Context: It becomes Earth's tactical center and plays a vital role in the Flameborn war effort.

Memory Flame

- Definition: The metaphysical energy generated by legacy, ancestral memory, and emotional resonance.

- Context: Central to Flameborn abilities and used to activate certain Zepharian devices like the Járnstóll core.

The Mirror

- Definition: A Voidborn agent that takes the form of one's deepest regrets or worst decisions.

- Context: Not a physical creature, but a psychic infiltrator encountered during breaches.

Mjölnar Protocol

- Pronunciation: *myol-nar*

- Definition: Earth's last-defense orbital weapon system named after Thor's hammer.

- Context: Deployed during the first large-scale Voidborn assault.

The Pale King

- Definition: A legendary Voidborn strategist said to have consumed three Zepharian moons.

- Context: A mythic-level threat possibly still dormant beyond the Bifrost system.

The Reclaimers

- Definition: A scattered group of Earth-based survivalists dedicated to rediscovering lost Zepharian tech.

- Context: Often seen as scavengers or tech-religionists; appear in Chapters 6 and 9.

Runeseal

- Definition: Security glyphs used to lock Zepharian interfaces from unauthorized access.

- Context: Can only be broken by specific DNA-resonant Flameborn or Zepharian permissions.

Runeskin

- Definition: A term for Zepharian-Viking neural implants activated in descendants.

- Context: Allows direct interaction with Zepharian tech and ancient memory locks.

Sigil Gate

- Definition: Personal teleportation rings used for Zepharian command units and high-ranking Flameborn.

- Context: Activated via thought-command and memory-flux signatures.

Svarthjarta

- Pronunciation: *svart-hyar-tah*

- Definition: The Black Heart; ancient Voidborn force representing entropy and oblivion.

- Context: The ultimate antagonist and cosmic threat to legacy itself.

Voidborn

- Definition: A race or entity from beyond known time and space, embodiments of entropy and oblivion.

- Context: The primary antagonistic force in the story; opposed by both humans and Zepharians.

The War-Mind

- Definition: A conscious shard of Svarthjarta able to infect and corrupt thought.

- Context: One of the greatest threats to Flameborn and human command units.

Appendix V: Timeline of Events

Timeline of *Norse Star*

9th Century — The Age of the Longships

856 AD — The Sky Breaks Open
Erik Bloodaxe and his fleet witness the arrival of a Zepharian
vessel during a mysterious aurora storm in the fjords of
Norway.
This marks First Contact.

858 AD — The Drakenskip Awakens
Zepharians gift Erik a hybrid ship bound to his bloodline.
Several warriors volunteer for an off-world journey,
becoming the first Flameborn.

860–1000 AD — The Disappearance

~865 AD — The Vanishing
Entire Viking strongholds across Norway vanish overnight.
Villages are abandoned. Only myths and runes remain.
The world forgets their departure.

2045 — The Modern Discovery

2045 — Dr. Astrid Jorgensen Uncovers the Fleet
A buried fleet of alien-Viking ships is discovered under Arctic
ice. The first preserved warrior is found—wearing armor not
of Earth.

2046 — Power Grid Collapse Across Scandinavia
Unusual aurorae herald the return of the Zepharians.
Massive orbs appear in the skies. Contact is reestablished.

2047 — The Flameborn Era

2047 — First Awakening of the Flameborn
Astrid and others of Norse descent begin manifesting runes
on their skin and latent memory powers. They are hunted,
studied, and eventually embraced as a new force.

2047 — The All-Thing Reclaimed
The Flameborn hold a modern version of the All-Thing to
unify awakened factions. Astrid is named Flamekeeper.
Freydis and Warborn break away.

2048 — Breach and Resistance

2048 — The Breach of Midgard
Voidborn forces infiltrate Earth via memory strain fractures.
Cities are overwhelmed by psychic resonance and corrupted
Flameborn.

2048 — Battle for the Bifrost Gate
Flameborn and Earth Resistance activate ancient
teleportation gates to evacuate survivors to Járnstóll Base.

2049 — Rise of the Void

2049 — The War-Mind Awakens
The Svarthjarta unleashes the War-Mind—a cognitive

destroyer that mimics grief and loss. Earth's orbiting
defenses collapse.

2050 — The Final War

2050 — The Siege of the Memory Core
Erik Bloodaxe, returned from deep galactic exile, leads the
Flameborn in a battle to defend the collective memory
archive of humanity.

2050 — The Last Stand of Midgard
A multi-factional defense of Earth ends with Erik's final
sacrifice and the temporary banishment of the Voidborn.

Appendix VI: Locations

TERRESTRIAL LOCATIONS

Fjordheim

- Type: Earth — Hidden valley near ancient Norwegian fjords

- Description: Birthplace of the Flameborn awakening; formerly Erik Bloodaxe's stronghold.

- Relevance: The location of the first Drakenskip launch.

- Key Events: First contact (Ch.1), Flameborn rituals (Ch.6)

- Status: Abandoned, restricted by global councils.

Tromsø Command (Járnstóll Base)

- Type: Earth — Arctic Command Fortress

- Description: Modern-day military-scientific base built atop Zepharian ruins.

- Relevance: Center for Flameborn recruitment, research, and last-stand coordination.

- Key Events: War-Mind breach defense (Ch.9), Flamekeeper ascension (Ch.11)

- Status: Active

The Veiled Ridge

- Type: Earth — Icelandic volcanic plateau

- Description: Believed to be where Zepharian memory anchors were buried.

- Relevance: A key site for vision quests and descendant trials.

- Key Events: Astrid's first memory fracture (Ch.6)

- Status: Geofenced by UN-Arkane treaties

INTERSTELLAR LOCATIONS

Aru-Ven System

- Type: Zepharian homeworld star cluster

- Description: Ancient binary star system with collapsing Dyson structures

- Relevance: Zepharian Prime's birthplace; site of old Flameborn cities

- Key Events: Mentioned in memory visions, target of Voidborn approach

- Status: Largely uninhabitable, under Zepharian preservation

---

Svarthjarta Rift

- Type: Extradimensional boundary

- Description: A tear between reality and the entropy space of the Voidborn

- Relevance: Central to Voidborn spawning and the War-Mind's network

- Key Events: Final chapters, Bifrost collapse

- Status: Unknown; constantly expanding

Járn-Sigmar Bastion

- Type: Orbital station in the Belt of Fire

- Description: Hybrid defense and archive satellite, built using Zepharian crystal architecture

- Relevance: Stores memory cores of Viking legacy

- Key Events: Final defense in Ch.16

- Status: Active, but partially corrupted post-War-Mind breach

---

The Bifrost Gate

- Type: Interstellar Portal

- Description: Network of ancient Zepharian transport rings aligned with memory pulses

- Relevance: Primary means of moving troops and data across galaxies

- Key Events: Siege in Ch.12, sacrifice of the Valkari

- Status: Severely damaged but partially functional

Appendix VII: Cultural Rituals & Beliefs

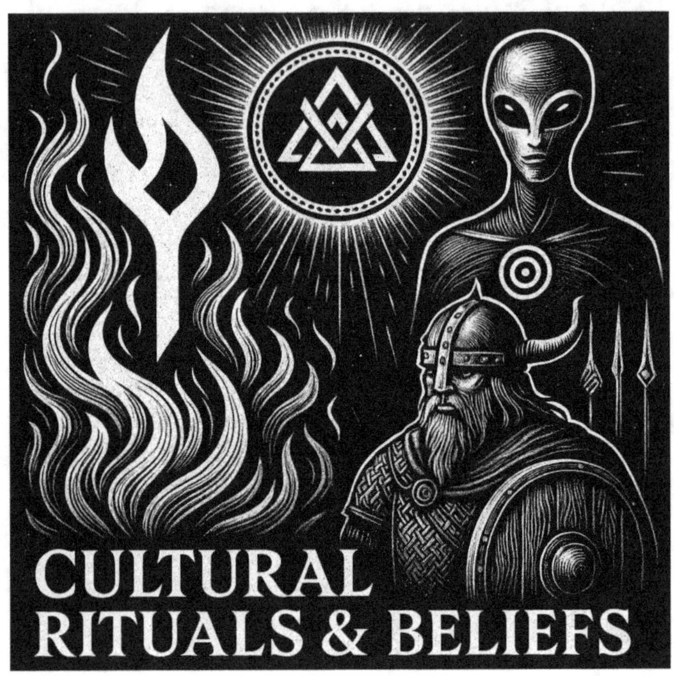

Rituals & Belief Systems

The Flamebond Rite

- Origin: Flameborn warrior tradition

- Participants: Two bonded warriors

- Purpose: A telepathic connection formed through memory flame sharing, linking two warriors' senses and emotions

- Symbolism: Eternal kinship; the unity of strength and vulnerability

- Appearance: Chapter 12 — Gunnar and Brynja

- Notes: Dangerous when performed in battle due to emotional overload

---

Memory Ascension

- Origin: Zepharian cultural philosophy

- Participants: Elder Zepharians, hybrid Flameborn

- Purpose: Transference of one's legacy into a collective memory hive before death

- Symbolism: Death is not an ending but transformation into wisdom

- Appearance: Chapter 9 and 14

- Notes: Some Flameborn fear this process as the loss of self

---

The All-Thing Reforged

- Origin: Norse tribal governance

- Participants: Clan leaders, Flameborn emissaries

- Purpose: A sacred gathering where decisions are made communally and symbolically reenacted through ritual combat or vision trials

- Symbolism: Balance of word and blade

- Appearance: Chapter 7 and 11

- Notes: Modernized under Astrid's leadership, integrating Zepharian elements

---

Ritual of the Sigil Veil

- Origin: Zepharian psionic protection rite

- Participants: Flameborn commanders

- Purpose: Shields minds from Voidborn psychic influence

- Symbolism: Trust in silence and inner strength

- Appearance: Chapter 10

- Notes: Leaves temporary blindness if miscast

The Forge Calling

- Origin: Hybrid culture — Zepharian forge-ritual merged with Norse rite of adulthood

- Participants: Young Flameborn at maturity

- Purpose: Binds warrior to their Forge-Stone, which crafts their weapon

- Symbolism: The soul shapes the blade

- Appearance: Chapter 8

- Notes: No two Forge-Stones are alike

Oath of the Shielded Flame

- Origin: New cultural synthesis post-Earth Awakening

- Participants: High Flameborn and Resistance leaders

- Purpose: Swearing loyalty to protect memory and kin

- Symbolism: The flame that guards, not devours

- Appearance: Chapter 13

- Notes: Can only be broken by ritual combat